A cryptic web of magic

The mist in Lady Jean's crystal hardened and began to pulse with new light. It took Jermyn by surprise, fastening sharp tendrils into the pathways of his mind, holding him hard. Frightened, he pulled against it and gasped as hot agony shot through him. . . .

Jermyn! Lady Jean's voice came from impossibly far away. *Don't try to pull. Cut it! Cut the thread!*

It was like being held by silvery spiderwebs that grew stronger every second. The glow at the center gathered strength, pulling all the strands of web into it; at its core, Jermyn dimly sensed, was a spreading stain of red against silver, as rich as soft velvet and as wet and warm as blood. Frantically, Jermyn fought against it, trying to focus. *Cut the thread? Which thread?* All he could see was haze.

The light flared, its heat flickering over him like rainwater. He watched, frozen, as the still-shimmering crystal rolled off the table . . . The brittle sound of glass breaking seemed to shiver through the entire tower as a great jagged piece chipped off one faceted side of the crystal and went spinning out into the center of the room.

JOURNEYMAN
WIZARD

MARY FRANCES
ZAMBRENO

Hyperion Paperbacks for Children
New York

First Hyperion Paperback edition 1996

First published in hardcover in 1994.
Reprinted by permission of Harcourt Brace and Company.

1 3 5 7 9 10 8 6 4 2

The text for this book is set in 12-point Garamond.

Library of Congress Cataloging-in-Publication Data
Zambreno, Mary Frances, (date)
Journeyman wizard : a magical mystery / Mary Frances Zambreno. —
1st Hyperion Paperback ed.
p.   cm.
Sequel to: A plague of sorcerers.
Summary: When Jermyn goes to Land's End to study wizardry under
the famous spellmaker Lady Jean Allons, he finds his lessons
disrupted by magical mayhem and a mysterious murder.
ISBN 0-7868-1127-7 (pbk.)
[1. Wizards—Fiction. 2. Magic—Fiction. 3. Mystery and
detective stories.] I. Title.
PZ7.Z2545Jo   1996
[Fic]—dc20   96-1264

In loving memory of my aunt,
Anna Calabrese,
who shared with me
the joys of a good mystery story.

And for my niece,
Sara Marie Zambreno,
who forgave me for renaming Brianne

CONTENTS

1

LAND'S END

JERMYN HAD his first look at the village of Land's End from on board the merchant ship *Dawn Voyager* as she sailed into the village harbor. He did not think much of it. Land's End was small, no more than a double curve of shoreline surrounded by gray stone buildings; only three fishing boats and a dinghy were moored alongside the little pier. The shore itself was deserted, unwelcoming even though drenched in midafternoon sunlight.

Get used to it, he told himself sternly. *This is going to be your home for however long it takes you to study with Lady Jean Allons. If you want to be a spellmaker, then you have to study with the Master Spellmaker, and this is where she lives.*

Beside him on the deck of the *Voyager*, his apprentice-master cleared his throat. "You can't see the village itself from here, you know," William Eschar said mildly. "It's farther inland, protected from the weather."

"Oh, I didn't realize," Jermyn said, relieved. He shivered slightly. "It is cold for early fall, isn't it?"

"Not really, not for this far north," Eschar told him. "Winters can be brutal up here. I hope your aunt told you to bring plenty of woolens."

"You know she did—you were there the *last* time she said it." William Eschar might be the Master Theoretician of the Wizards' Guild, but he'd obviously been of secondary importance on the day that Merovice Graves bid her nephew farewell.

"Now, you're sure you packed your heavy cloak?" she'd fussed. "Why aren't you wearing your woolen tunic? Where's your hood?"

"It's right here," Jermyn had reassured her for what felt like the tenth time. He was a little embarrassed; you'd think he was a child, not almost seventeen and a nearly journeyman-class wizard.

"Then put it on!" she'd snapped at him. "You can't learn to be a spellmaker if you're always coming down with pleurisy or pneumonia. Precious few healers up in that northwoods wilderness, too, I suppose. Don't forget to eat your green vegetables,

2

especially in winter—and be sure to keep Delia indoors. You know how country people are about skunks."

Remembering her last comment, Jermyn frowned. Delia was his wizard's familiar, the animal that allowed him to use his own inborn abilities to pull magical power from the natural world. She was also a skunk. He loved her, but there was no denying she tended to cause problems. Most familiars were cats or birds of prey; any other animal was considered unusual. A skunk was worse than unusual—it was downright peculiar.

Right now, Delia was securely locked into a spelled carry-case resting at his feet. He sent an inquiring tendril of thought at her—yes, she was awake, but she wouldn't talk to him. *Probably sulking,* he thought to himself. *She does hate that case.*

Suddenly Jermyn needed reassurance. "Master Eschar, do you think Delia will be all right? Country people are so superstitious about skunks being bad luck."

Eschar was filling his pipe with tobacco, though how he meant to light it in this wind Jermyn couldn't guess. "It may be difficult," he admitted. "Particularly if Delia manages to get into the sort of trouble she always seems to stumble into so innocently at home. Still, I think it will work out. When I lived up here as Lady Jean's student, I got to know the locals fairly well. They won't interfere with a practicing wizard, or with his familiar. Just be discreet and everything will be fine. We *have* discussed all this, you know, Jermyn. Don't tell me you've forgotten."

"Of course not," Jermyn said, slightly indignant. After Lady Jean's message had come, he and Master Eschar had talked at length about Land's End and its spellmaker Lady.

"So Mistress Allons is Lady of the Manor as well as Master Spellmaker?" Jermyn had asked as he cleaned out his desk in Master Eschar's library. Outside, it was a warm day in early autumn. Delia was curled up asleep in the sunlight that streaked through the tall library windows.

"Yes, she is," the Theoretician answered from his side of the room. "Once upon a time, her son and I were students together, but he entered the Church several years ago. Her daughter married and had one child, a girl who would be about your age by now, I imagine, or perhaps a year or two younger. Lady Jean's daughter died—in an accident." He paused, his jaw setting slightly. "A tragic, *magical* accident. Such things can happen to wizards who don't take proper care."

"Yes, sir." Jermyn nodded soberly. "I know."

"Well . . . you will find Jean a strict taskmaster, I imagine," Eschar went on. "She takes her craft very seriously. When I lived with her, she had several general students, but since then she's said she'll teach only spellmakers. Of whom you are the first the Guild has been able to find, and the only one she's accepted, for years."

"I'll work hard, I promise," Jermyn said, grinning. Then his grin faded. "Was it very difficult, living up north with Lady Jean?"

The Theoretician hesitated. "It had its moments. Looking back, I can't say it was easy—but it seems that I remember only the good parts. That's natural, I suppose. Why? Are you worried about living so far from the city?"

Jermyn squirmed. "Not worried, exactly. Not about living in Land's End. I expect it'll be boring, but I can handle that. Only, what's she *really* like? Lady Jean, I mean."

"Ah, I thought that might be it," Eschar said. He rubbed one finger behind his ear and smiled reflectively. "Well, she's stern, but she's also a very good teacher, and as warm and generous as her Power. She has a rather dry sense of humor that may take some getting used to, but she never jokes about sorcery. Or about scholarship. I think you will learn a great deal from her—once you get over being scared of her shadow."

"Scared?" Jermyn said. "Why should I be scared? I'm not a little boy in dame school."

"Neither was I, when I went north," Eschar

said, amused. "And I was frightened out of my wits."

On the deck of the *Dawn Voyager*, Jermyn put the memory from him.

"Of course I haven't forgotten," he repeated firmly. "I was only making conversation."

"I didn't think that you had forgotten, really," Eschar said soothingly. "I know how good a memory you have—especially for spells. Is Master Morrenthau's shielding on Delia's case still holding?"

As a theoretical wizard—*the* Master Theoretician of the Guild—William Eschar had no practical ability in magic. Since he could neither cast nor see a spell, he had to rely on his apprentice for information about such matters.

"It seems to be," Jermyn answered, squinting at the case and its interlocking weave of bindings. "I can tell Dee is in there, but I don't think anyone else could—especially not another animal that might panic at the sight or scent of a skunk. The pattern's sort of strange looking, though. It looks like a magical birdcage."

"Probably it was developed as something like that," Eschar mused, watching the sailors tie the *Voyager* fast to its mooring. "Morrenthau told me he'd never been called on to do anything quite like this before, and he had to adapt a spell originally created for a different purpose."

"Yes, sir," Jermyn said. Adapting the old spell had been easier than creating a new one, particularly since Lady Jean had been retired from formal spell-making for several years. *Someday, adapting creaky old spells won't be necessary,* he vowed privately. *Someday, when I'm a master spellmaker, I'll make all-new spells whenever people need them, so no one will have to rely on changing old ones to fit the circumstances.*

In her case, Delia stirred slightly. *Good Je'm'n,* she said. *Good Je'm'n make strong magic.*

Well, hello again, he said, blushing a little at the praise in her mind-voice. Sometimes, Jermyn wished he were half as sure of himself as Delia was of him. *I'm glad you approve. Are you comfortable in there?*

She blew him a soft mental raspberry. *No.*

"That's it, they have secured the gangplank," Eschar said, turning. "And I think I see our carriage over by the customs house. Come along, Jermyn."

"Yes, sir." Hastily, he picked up Delia's case.

Eschar was already down the gangplank, walking with long strides toward a black carriage waiting on the quay. Jermyn hurried to catch up.

"Phineas?" Eschar called, knocking on the side panel. "Are you there?"

A tall, muffled form slouched around the carriage. "Master William?"

"Yes, it's me," Eschar said, shaking the man's hand vigorously. "Jermyn, this is Lady Jean's coachman and my old friend, Phineas Mayhew. Phin, this is Jermyn Graves, my apprentice and now Lady Jean's journeyman."

Phineas was thin and wiry. His face was lined with age, but his callused grip was strong enough to make Jermyn swallow hard. "Welcome t'Land's End, Young Master. We'd best be moving."

"I'm not a master," Jermyn said, startled, but Eschar shushed him.

"We'll be off as soon as you can load our bags, Phineas," he said. "Do you need any help?"

The old man looked slightly insulted. "Brought t'whole city north wi' ye? I can manage, Master William. Allus have."

He got the bags loaded faster than Jermyn would have thought possible, slinging them up onto the carriage roof and lashing them into place. When he reached for Delia's case, Jermyn stopped him.

"This is my familiar," he said. "She goes inside with us."

Phineas nodded and spit into the road. "Fair 'nough. Let's go, then."

When the carriage had started to move, Jermyn turned to Master Eschar. "Why did you let him call me 'Young Master'? I'm not a master. I won't even be a journeyman until Lady Jean formally accepts me."

"It's an old country habit up here in the Northernmost Province," the Theoretician said. "Any magic-worker is called 'Master' or 'Mistress,' whether or not that's the appropriate Guild rank. Don't worry, you'll soon become accustomed."

Jermyn turned to the window. There wasn't much to see; they were already passing the last houses in the village by the time he looked for it. "I thought you said there was more of the village than we could see from the ship," he remarked. "It doesn't look like much from up close, either."

Eschar chuckled. "Not impressed, are you? Well, I suppose any country town would look small after the city. Wait until we get where we're going. That should satisfy you."

The carriage picked up speed. Jermyn grabbed for a strap as the horses started going uphill. "How far *are* we going?"

"Tower Landing is just outside the village proper, in the center of a small farmhold," Eschar said. "You'll be able to see it soon."

In a few minutes, Jermyn saw its shadow; then a great stone bulk loomed over the horizon. Lady Jean's tower reached up higher than most city monuments. Made of the same dark stone as the cliffs behind it, the building looked like a work of nature. Running east along the ground was a wing of about two stories, altogether dwarfed by the mass beside it.

"Powers Below," Jermyn said in awe. "Who built that?"

"Lady Jean's ancestor, the first Lord of Land's End," Eschar said. "Or rather, he started it and his widow finished it. People had need of strong shelters when they first came to this land."

Delia's black nose poked against the mesh air holes of her case.

Want out, she grumbled. *Can't see. Can't smell.*

Pretty soon, he said soothingly. *Just be patient, and you'll be able to see and smell as much as you want.*

Outside the carriage, Phineas's voice called to the horses, "Whoa, there! Good boys—whoa!"

"There, that didn't take long," Eschar said, reaching to open the door. "Well done, Phineas. You made good time."

The carriage had stopped in a covered entrance with shallow stone steps leading to a great wooden door.

"Horses wanted t'get home before snow," the coachman said.

"Snow?" Eschar sniffed the air as he waited for Jermyn to get out of the carriage after him. "Is it going to snow?"

" 'Tis." Phineas grinned, showing widely spaced

yellow teeth. "You lose all your weather sense shut up in the city, Master William?"

"I'm afraid so," Eschar said, smiling.

Jermyn leaned closer. The sky was clear blue, with only a few clouds; it didn't look like snow to him. "Is he a weather wizard?"

"No. He just smelled snow in the air," Eschar said, as if it were the most natural thing in the world. He reached for the iron door knocker. "Country people live close to the weather. They learn to sense such things."

The door swung slowly inward. A tall man with thin brown hair and faded blue eyes stood facing them. He was wearing a stitched blue tunic that matched his eyes and made his face look sallow; his pointed nose reminded Jermyn of a ferret's. He looked from Jermyn to Master Eschar, then settled on the Theoretician as the one more worthy of his attention.

"Who are you?" he asked, drawing himself up officiously. "What do you want?"

Eschar raised his eyebrows. "Good day. I'm Guild Master Theoretician William Eschar, and this is my apprentice, Jermyn Graves. I believe we're expected."

The door swung wider. "Expected? What do you—was that old Phineas, with the carriage?"

"It was," Eschar said. "He met us at the harbor."

11

The man frowned. *He looks even more like a ferret that way,* Jermyn thought irrepressibly, then squelched the thought sternly. "I'm Duncan Campbell. I wasn't told we were having visitors."

"Ah, yes, then you'll be Jean's son-in-law," Eschar said, smoothly pushing his way into the front hall. Jermyn followed him gratefully; it was cold outside. "I don't believe we've met."

"Why should we have met?" Duncan asked, sounding confused. Behind him, a massive wooden staircase curved along the inner wall, its dark wood mellow in the sunlight. "Look, if you're here to see my mother-in-law, I'm afraid you'll have to wait. She's resting. She always rests in the afternoon."

"Duncan?" a woman's voice said from the stairs. "Who is there?"

"I'm sorry, Mother, I didn't mean to disturb—"

"It's William, Mistress Allons," Eschar said, speaking over him. "I've brought you your new journeyman."

"Of course." She moved into the light, and Jermyn gaped at his first sight of the woman who was to be his journeyman-master—the Guild's most powerful spellmaker and the *only* master spellmaker in the Wizards' Guild for as long as anyone could remember. He wasn't sure what he'd been expecting, but now he knew: *This* was what a spellmaker should look like.

Lady Jean was a tall woman, with silver hair curling softly around a stern face. Her eyes were deep blue and very bright; she wore a sapphire silk dress, and earrings that exactly matched its shade. Although her features were lined with age, her gaze was level and penetrating and her chin was very firm. She looked—*elegant* was the best word, Jermyn decided. As elegant and graceful as a length of polished steel. She used a cane as she came down the stairs, but her step was steady—measured, not slow. Beside her, a young girl with sandy blond hair stood half in shadow.

"Welcome, William," the spellmaker said, her eyes on Master Eschar. "Welcome back to Tower Landing. Duncan, don't keep our guests standing in the hallway. Bring them in."

Campbell was annoyed. "Why wasn't I told they were coming?"

"Because you've been out west, overseeing the harvest," she said from the foot of the staircase. The girl at her elbow moved with her, leaning forward as if ready to offer support but holding back until she was needed. "We weren't certain they'd get through before the winter storms set in. But you always did have a good sense of timing, didn't you, William?"

Almost as tall as Master Eschar, she stopped before him and offered her cheek for him to kiss. Gallantly, he greeted her.

13

"So you've always said, My Lady." He smiled at her, real affection in his face. "I must admit, I've never noticed, myself."

"Tut, of course you wouldn't." She returned his smile, but there was something strained about her, Jermyn thought—almost as if she were forcing herself to look cheerful. Then she turned to look at the other new arrival. "And so this is Jermyn Graves."

Gulping, he stepped forward and bowed as deeply as he could, with Delia's case bumping his legs. "Yes, ma'am. Lady Jean."

"You will call me Mistress Allons, until I tell you otherwise," she said, inspecting him as if he were a specimen in a glass jar.

"Yes, ma'am—Mistress Allons," he said, almost stuttering. He could feel the blood rising in his cheeks. Helplessly, he looked at Master Eschar, but the Theoretician seemed wholly preoccupied by his own thoughts.

"It's been too long, Jean," Eschar said, shaking his head. "Much too long. Are we in the east wing? Or did you put us in the tower itself?"

Lady Jean's attention left Jermyn as if he'd melted into a puddle on the floor; he almost wished that he had. "In the tower, on the second floor. Old Phineas should have your bags up to your rooms by now. Won't you have a cup of tea with me before you unpack?"

"With pleasure," Eschar said. "In the library?"

"Of course," she said lightly. "As if I could keep you out of it for long! Is it true you've retired yourself?"

"Yes, for the most part," he said, shrugging. "Princess Alexandra will hardly need my advice until she grows up. I still take an occasional client for old times' sake, though. And naturally I have not given up my studies."

"Naturally not," she said. "I've recently acquired several volumes that you might wish to inspect . . . if you aren't too tired from your voyage."

"Too tired to look at books?" Eschar said briskly. "Never! I think Jermyn had best be occupied in getting his familiar settled in, though."

"Jermyn? Yes, of course. Brianne, will you show Mr. Graves his rooms? Then come to me in the library." With a flick of the wrist she dismissed both Jermyn and his familiar.

"Yes, Gran," the girl replied obediently.

"Duncan, bring us the new-purchases catalog, please," Jean went on.

"Certainly, Mother," Campbell said. He ignored Jermyn, too.

Together, Campbell, Lady Jean, and Master Eschar disappeared around the stairs, going through broad double doors that silently closed behind them.

For a moment, Jermyn felt completely abandoned. Then a soft voice said from beside him, "If you'd follow me, please."

He jumped. He'd forgotten the girl. As she moved into the light, he could see that her hair was thick and soft; she wore it braided at the back of her head. Her eyes were more gray-blue than blue, not as vivid as Lady Jean's.

She returned his look calmly, with no sign that she'd noticed his inspection.

"Uh—I'm sorry. I didn't—" He stopped himself; he was babbling. *She's pretty*, he thought. *And not* that *much younger than I am. Fourteen—maybe even fifteen, I'd guess.* He liked the way the little tendrils of hair escaping around her face caught the light. "Excuse me. I—uh—I'm afraid I didn't hear your name."

"I'm Brianne Campbell," she said, gravely. "Duncan Campbell is my father and Lady Jean is my grandmother. My mother is dead."

"Oh. I—that is, I'm Jermyn Graves." He swallowed, annoyed at his stuttering. *She knows that, dummy.* He was not making a good showing here.

She smiled, courteous but cool. "Gran did say I was to take you to your rooms. Or would you rather stand here in the hall all day?"

"No, of course not," he said, taking a fresh grip on Delia's case. He cast one look of burning reproach in the direction that Master Eschar had gone, and then he followed Brianne up the stairs.

"You're in the main tower, by Gran's workroom," she said over her shoulder. "A fire has been burning in it all day, so it should be warm."

"Thank you," he said, moving up beside her as she started down a long hallway. The floor was inlaid stone, its intricate pattern faded with much time and use. On the walls, dark wood paneling gleamed. "I would like to freshen up and let my familiar out."

"Is that what you've got in the case?" she asked, stopping in front of a door. "I wondered why you were hanging on to it so."

"Yes, it is," he said, pleased at her interest. "I hope she gets along with Lady Jean's familiar."

Brianne glanced at him curiously. "Gran hasn't had a familiar since I was a little girl."

"What?" Jermyn frowned. *A practicing wizard without a familiar? Of course, she's not active in the Guild—but how does she work magic?*

"That's right." As she swung the door wide, she didn't even seem conscious that she'd said something strange; Jermyn decided not to comment—not just yet. "Here we are. The maids will need to get in to clean, of course, but otherwise this is your place. They all know better than to disturb a working wizard."

Jermyn set Delia's case down on the floor. His suitcases and trunk were piled along the other wall, in front of a tall wardrobe between two windows. A fire burned in the hearth.

Brianne pointed to a door facing the bed. "The water closet is through there, and the dressing room. There should be fresh water in the basin. If there isn't, pull the bell cord for one of the maids—she'll bring it. Your private workroom is on the other side of the dressing room. Dinner is at six, and you'll want to dress. Is there anything else you need?"

"No, thank you," he said politely.

She nodded. "See you at dinner, then. Don't be late—Gran hates it when people are late."

The door closed behind her. Jermyn sat down on the bed, feeling drained. "Well! So dinner is at six and I'll want to dress, will I?"

Want out, Delia said imperatively, nosing the front mesh. Her black nose poked through the webbing. *Want out now!*

"All right, I'm letting you out," he said, snapping the latches. "Behave. Lady Jean didn't look like she'd laugh at you if you got in trouble. Not like Master Eschar."

She sniffed disdainfully, her eyes bright as she stalked out of the case. *Huh. Silly Je'm'n talk-talk too much.*

In fact, Jermyn thought dismally, Lady Jean wasn't like Master Eschar at all. He'd only known her a few minutes, and already he knew that he didn't want to displease her. Probably no one did.

She looks—imperious, he thought uneasily. *Like a Ruling Princess. What if she doesn't like me? Well, it could be worse—she could be as rude as the son-in-law. The granddaughter seems nice. Cool, though. Maybe she's been told not to get too friendly with students. Brianne. That's a pretty name.* He sighed. *I guess Lady Jean doesn't have to like me, anyway, so long as she lets me study with her.*

The door Brianne had pointed out led to a connecting hallway with a water closet on one side. On the other side there was a walk-in clothes closet, and another door. Jermyn opened it and found a small but complete workroom. There was a desk much like his old one in Master Eschar's library, a display case, and bookshelves with a few new workbooks sitting on them. Jermyn picked one up: The place on the cover for the student's name was blank. *She must have ordered this room made ready for me,* he thought. *I'm her only student. Why didn't she have my name put on the workbooks when she got them from the stationer, like Master Eschar always did?* He said aloud, "Maybe she isn't really sure about me. . . ."

He shut the workbook with a snap and put it back on the shelf. "Oh, don't be silly," he scolded himself. *She probably just had some old workbooks lying around and couldn't be bothered to write my name in them herself. She's certainly got more important things to do.*

He went back to the dressing room and made use of the basin there gratefully, splashing water on his hands and face; he'd been feeling pretty grimy from traveling. *Aunt Merry should see me now,* he thought with amusement. *After all the years she's had to remind me to wash behind my ears.* The thought of his aunt brought a pang of homesickness, which he pushed out of his mind. At the last moment, he checked his hair in the mirror and decided it would do.

Back out in the bedroom, he debated dressing for dinner and decided it was too early. The clothes he was wearing were clean enough for a little exploring, and he was curious about this house and its great tower. Maybe he could even look around outside, though the sky through the windows had turned dark. It really did look like snow now, just as old Phineas had said.

"Deedee? Want to go for a walk?"

Only then did he realize that the hall door was slightly ajar and that Delia was nowhere to be seen. Frantically, he checked the room, searching with his eyes and through the magical link in his mind. Both agreed.

Delia was gone.

2

THE HEDGEWITCH

IT WAS his own fault, he realized as he stood in the open doorway. He'd only told her to behave; he hadn't told her not to leave the room. And Delia was very good at jiggling unlocked doors open.

If she surprises one of the servants, it could be terrible, he thought, feeling sick to his stomach. *Or if Lady Jean keeps dogs, it could be worse—no, I don't have time to think about what could happen. I've got to find her before anything does happen.*

He took a deep breath and closed his eyes to concentrate. *She can't have gone far*, he thought, trying to calculate how long it had been since he'd let her out of the case. *Delia? Deedee, where are you?*

Cold. She was someplace cold. He clenched one fist reflexively and strained to listen. Someplace cold and filled with rustling shadows . . .

Oh no! She's outside somewhere. And if half of what I've heard about country people and skunks is true, she could be in real danger.

He grabbed his cloak and headed for the stairs, trying to plan. *I could call her back, but that might take too long. She could get into just as much trouble finding her way home alone as she could wandering around. I'd better go fetch her.*

The hall was empty, and so was the entryway. When he opened the front door, a blast of cold wind almost pushed him back to the foot of the stairs.

It was snowing.

He stood for a moment, looking out. Beyond the carriageway was a dark wood, made darker now by the weather. Delia's mental call was coming from there. If he left the road, he'd be lost in minutes. But if he didn't, he might not find Delia.

A noise in the hall decided him. Fastening his cloak tightly, he plunged into the cold. Behind him, the door swung shut slowly.

The great bulk of Tower Landing loomed over everything. If he could keep that stone mass in sight, he'd be all right. But once under the trees he could scarcely see the sky. New-fallen snow was beginning to collect on the ground; he brushed stinging particles away from his face and concentrated on the golden cord in his mind that linked him to his familiar.

Delia? Dark and cold, yes, I know that. Which way? He reached out, feeling the magic trickle into him like sunlight. *Straight ahead, then a little left —that way, under those big pine trees.*

The wind died down as he walked deeper into the woods. The underbrush was thin at first, but it got thicker and harder to struggle through the farther he went. Finally he had to stop and hunt out a walking stick from the deadfalls littering the way. Constantly, he called, both with his mind and his mouth: *Delia, Delia, where is Delia?* "Come out, Dee, wherever you are."

He scanned the ground ahead of him as he walked, wishing for more light. Even on a bright, sunny afternoon, not much light would get through these branches. Then he saw a patch of darkness that wasn't quite the same shade as the ground, scuttling toward him. He pounced, picking her up. "Dee! Bad girl, where have you been?"

She lifted her head and chortled at him. *Come see, Je'm'n,* she said, her mind-voice delighted. *Come see funny magic.*

"What do you mean, funny magic?" he scolded her, his fear for her giving way to indignation. "You know better than to wander around a strange place all on your own. What did I tell you before we left home?"

Je'm'n mad? She twisted to peer up at him. *Didn't say, stay warm-dry.*

"Of course I'm angry," he said, as sternly as he could. "I may not have told you to stay indoors, but you shouldn't have left the room without telling me you were going—and you must have scampered to get this far."

Aww. . . . She lowered her pointed nose until it fell almost between her forepaws, the perfect picture of misery. *So sorry Je'm'n mad.*

"Now cut that out! I know perfectly well you don't mean it."

Immediately she perked up. *Come see funny magic, Je'm'n,* she repeated brightly. *All smelly.*

"What are you talking about?" he asked her, puzzled. She sent a wave of psychic odors at him, spicy and thick with smoke. He gagged. "What's that?"

Squirming, she jumped out of his arms to the ground. *Smelly magic. Come see.* She trotted off between two evergreens, her bushy tail twitching behind her. When he didn't follow at once, she paused and looked back at him. *Je'm'n?*

"All right, all right, I'm coming," he said, wondering what she was up to now. Apparently, something in the woods had drawn her; he probably ought to find out what it was before they went back. "We shouldn't go too far, though."

Not far, she promised. *See?*

A clearing opened out in front of her. In it was a small hut with a snowy thatched roof. A ragged little terrier growled from around one side of the place; then the dog scented Delia and yiped, disappearing with its tail down. Delia looked smug. *Smelly,* she said.

"What's smelly? The dog? Look, I know you don't like dogs, but that's no reason to go around spooking them." She planted her paws firmly and looked up at him commandingly. "Oh, all right." Obediently, he took a deep breath. "I don't smell anything—wait a minute. Yes, I do."

Magic. He couldn't have explained what he smelled, or how. It wasn't really an odor, though he often talked with Delia about magic in terms of smelling—she seemed to understand him better that way. This was more like a whisper of fragrance in the mind. And this smell-that-was-not-a-smell in the cool dark woods was an odd one, almost reminding him of going into Merovice's workroom when she was preparing the stronger spells that went with her healing herbs. Almost, but not quite. When Aunt Merry used magic, it was fresh, like clear water or a morning breeze. This strange tang was old and not too clean, and there was a burned feel to it, like vegetables that had been left too long in a boiling pot. Hesitantly, he tried to trace the source lines, to see what sort of spell was being constructed. All he got was mush.

Well, it's coming from the hut, of course—must be, he thought. *I could just go ask what it is. But it's dangerous to interrupt someone doing magic, especially someone you don't know. I wonder if Lady Jean knows what's going on? She should. This is pretty close to her tower.*

Delia poked his foot peremptorily; she wanted him to go ask about the smelly magic. Before he could make up his mind, the door to the hut opened, letting out a flood of brightness that made him wince.

"Eh? Who's there?" asked a very old voice.

The odd magic faded. Jermyn took a deep breath. "I'm sorry to intrude," he called to the hut's owner. "I was just passing by."

The door opened wider. He heard a second voice mumble something urgently in the background, but he couldn't make out the words. The first voice ignored it. "Who's come to see old Maudie?"

He swallowed. "I'm Jermyn Graves. I'm—uh—I'm staying at the Tower, with Mistress Allons," he said, squinting into the light.

Outlined by the fire stood an old woman wearing a black wool dress, very heavy and coarse, and a faded head kerchief that looked like it was older than

Jermyn. Her eyes, black and small in her wrinkled face, looked him over from crown to toes. She frowned when she saw Delia peering out from behind Jermyn's legs.

"Well, come in, come in, then," she said, turning away. "No use standin' out getting wetter and colder. Come in, and bring in that silly beast that frighted my Towser, too."

Towser must be the dog, Jermyn thought as he bent and picked up Delia. She snuggled cheerfully into his arms. *Funny,* she said happily. *Go see.*

We're stuck seeing now, he told her, setting his walking stick down by the door. Inside, he stood for a moment to get his bearings. The interior of the hut was messy and filled with smoke from the central hearth fire. The old woman—Maudie?—had her back turned to him as she fussed with an ancient iron kettle.

Brianne Campbell was sitting on a stool next to the hearth.

Jermyn blinked. "What are you doing here?"

"I could ask the same of you," she snapped, twisting her hands together in her lap. The distantly polite girl who had led him to his room had vanished; *this* Brianne was stretched as tight and tense as—as an overworked spell, Jermyn thought. Then she saw Delia in his arms. "And where did you get *that?*"

"She's my registered Guild familiar," Jermyn

said, a little stiffly. *Why is she so nervous? This is her grandmother's estate, and she has every right to be here. So do I, if I want to be.* He couldn't help the stir of mild resentment he felt at her question—and at her attitude toward Delia. "You saw her case earlier. I—um, I was just taking her for a walk when we saw this place. . . ."

She didn't seem to notice his evasion. "I thought your familiar was a cat. You brought a *skunk* with you from the city? Does Gran know?"

"I assume so," he told her. "Master Eschar has written to her about me, after all. I suppose she—she just didn't bother to mention it to anyone."

"I suppose so," Brianne said. "I can't believe it. Who ever heard of a wizard having a skunk for a familiar?"

"Familiars can be any meat-eating animal," he said, trying not to be *too* annoyed. After all, he had heard it all before. "Just because they're mostly cats or birds of prey doesn't mean they always have to be."

"Sa, sa, don't jangle," Maudie said, turning away from the hearth with the kettle in her hands. "Sit down, city boy, you and that devil's child you're holdin'. The stool's waitin' for you."

There was a second stool by the fire. Jermyn ignored it. "Delia is my familiar," he repeated, his eyes on the old woman. "Properly registered. Any-one who harms her will answer to the Wizards' Guild. In force."

Maudie grinned, showing broken brown teeth. "A Guild boy, is it? Afraid old Maudie'll make her-sel' some skunk stew? Well, so you should be. Tasty, skunk stew is, though most folks don't think it. Tender as squirrel. Oh, sit down, sit down. No need to fear old Maudie."

"Yes, sit down, Jermyn," Brianne said. "Unless you'd rather just leave."

He *did* want to leave, but there didn't seem to be any way of doing it without being rude. Looking suspiciously from Brianne to Maudie, Jermyn sank onto the other stool and accepted a thick mug of steaming liquid. Taking his first swallow, he almost choked. The tea was hot, strong, and salty with butter. He glared at Brianne, who was placidly drinking hers.

"You'll get used to it," she said. "It's quite pop-ular in the village."

Delia sniffed his mug with interest. He wished he dared offer it to her, but Maudie was looking right at him. Meekly, he took another sip.

"So, you're for Missy Jeanie," Maudie said abruptly. "Well 'nough. She needs a young 'un, this end."

"Huh?" Jermyn said, spraying buttered tea all down the front of his cloak. "What did you—do you mean *Mistress Allons?*"

"I mean what I do say," Maudie said mysteri-ously. Her black eyes glittered. "I'm old, city boy.

I've lived hereabouts as long as the land itself, and the Power is mine by right."

All at once, the hut and the old woman and the odd smell of magic in the woods added up, and he was embarrassed that he hadn't understood before. "You're a hedgewitch," he said incredulously.

"She's the village wisewoman," Brianne tartly corrected him. "She has been for years."

"That's only another word for it," Jermyn said heatedly.

"Wisewoman I am," Maudie said, nodding placidly. "An' m'mother an' m'gran'mother before me."

Jermyn bit his tongue on a sharp answer. Hedgewitches were natural magic-workers; they tended to scrabble for a living in remote areas, generally trying to avoid official notice. The Guild did not think highly of them, but there were always a few around, even in the city. Mostly they told cheap fortunes or sold highly suspect love potions to the gullible and not-too-intelligent.

"That's so, they were," Brianne said, her voice cold as the wind outside.

Abruptly Jermyn realized that he was currently *this* hedgewitch's guest, and that she did seem to have a certain amount of real talent. It had been genuine sorcery that had led him to the hut. Such untrained magic was, at best, unpredictable. At worst, it could be dangerous. He shouldn't risk getting Maudie angry with him or with Delia. Or with

Brianne, for that matter, though the girl seemed to feel perfectly at home here.

"Ah—greetings, Mistress," he said to Maudie at last, almost choking on the formal title. Brianne smiled grimly. "Then—you'd be the source of the magic spell that my familiar and I followed into the woods?"

"Eh?" For a moment, the hedgewitch seemed confused, and Jermyn realized how very old she must be. Brianne went white; she opened her mouth to say something, but Maudie spoke first. "What d'you mean, spell?"

"My familiar and I sensed someone working magic in the woods," he explained. "Someone around this hut. We were wondering what it was."

Funny smell, Delia repeated, looking up in bright curiosity. Privately he hushed her.

"Oh, that," Brianne said, not looking at him. "That was nothing. Just—just something Maudie was doing when I got here."

Maudie nodded, her eyes gleaming oddly. She looked from Brianne to Jermyn, and back again. "So. A spell you'd call it, such as you are, but 'tis only power—power from the earth an' the fire. Power for the teachin' witchery, like m'mother an' m'gran'mother before me. . . ."

She bent over the hearth as if to dismiss the subject, settling the kettle firmly on the banked fire again. Genuinely shocked, Jermyn turned to

Brianne. "*Teaching* witchery? Brianne, you don't mean *you*—"

Looking desperate, Brianne stood up. "Maudie? Is there anything you'd like me to bring next time?"

Maudie didn't look up from the fire. "Bring sugar. 'Tis cold and dark, winter, an' sweet stuff's good for Power in the cold and dark."

"I don't think I can get sugar. How about honey?"

The old woman frowned. "Sugar's better."

"All right, I'll try to get sugar," she said. "But I have to leave now."

"Uh-huh." She glanced once, measuringly, at Jermyn. He stirred uneasily under the sharp gaze, feeling himself weighed by some standard that he didn't understand, but the hedgewitch didn't speak to him again. Instead, she turned back to Brianne. "You do that, Missy. You do that, for fair."

"Until—until then, Mistress," Brianne said. She grabbed Jermyn's arm and almost pulled him out of the hut. He followed her willingly; the cold was cleansing, after even a short time in the stuffy closeness of the hut. He stood by the door for a moment, pulling fresh air into his lungs.

Down? Delia said hopefully.

"No, you don't," he told her, and put her on his shoulder to ride back. He winced as her blunt claws pressed through his cloak, and he wished he'd taken the time to search out and tie on the leather shoulder pad he normally used when he carried her. "I don't want to lose you again."

"We'd better hurry," Brianne said. She had already started for the edge of the clearing. "We're going to be late for dinner. Besides, Towser's about somewhere, and that dog gets pretty vicious with people he doesn't know." *Like you*, her tone finished the sentence.

"Don't worry about the dog," he told her. "He won't bother us. Delia took care of him. Look, Brianne, we've got to talk about what just happened."

"What do you mean?" she said, walking a little faster. "I already told you, Maudie is the village wisewoman."

"Yes, and she told me that she's teaching someone witchery—read, *magic*," he said, catching up. Delia protested at the pace, jouncing on his shoulder, but he ignored her. "And since you were the only person in there for her to be teaching, and since she seemed to be giving you instructions about what to do 'next time' . . ."

He let the sentence drift away. Brianne stood still for a long moment, then whirled to face him. "All right, so she's teaching me magic. What about it?"

"You're learning magic from a hedgewitch? As

her apprentice?" When he said it out loud, it sounded ridiculous; people didn't *apprentice* to hedgewitches. "Does your *grandmother* know?"

"Of course not," she said. "But I have to—there just isn't anyone else."

"Mistress Allons—"

"Gran won't teach me," she interrupted him. "Or maybe she can't. She says I'm not a spellmaker and that's the only kind of wizard she'll teach anymore—a spellmaker, like you. And Father won't let me go to school in the city. Won't hear of my studying magic, period." She was almost spitting the words. "Even Uncle Eben just says I'm too young to know my own mind. Well, Maudie doesn't think I'm too young."

"You *are* young," he said, unwilling to take the hedgewitch's opinion on anything.

"I'm fourteen," she snapped. "Almost fifteen. I'll bet I'm as old as you were when you became an apprentice."

"Well . . . not quite," he said, and stopped, remembering what it was like before he'd become an apprentice. He'd wanted to be a real wizard, a Guild wizard, so much that he couldn't think of anything else. He'd even practiced working Aunt Merry's crystal, so he'd be ready when the day finally came. Fourteen wasn't too young to enter the Guild. It was certainly old enough to dream about the future. "I was kind of late. It's as old as most apprentices, though, you're right. Why won't your father let you study magic?"

The fire drained out of her. "My mother. She was a wizard, like Uncle Eben was going to be before he became a priest. Then, one day, she had an accident, and she—died."

"Master Eschar told me about the accident," Jermyn said. He didn't have to work to put sympathy into his voice. "He didn't give me any of the details, though."

"I can tell you about it, if you really want to know," Brianne said, visibly taking herself in hand.

Jermyn nodded. "If you don't mind."

"Mother was adapting a spell, as an experiment. After she got back from her apprenticeship in the city, she used to help Gran a lot, so I guess she thought she could do more to the spell than she should have—even though she wasn't a spellmaker. Anyway, something went wrong, and she died. I was just a baby, so I don't remember her at all. But Gran hasn't done any serious magic since that day, and Father . . ." Her voice trailed off, and she turned and started walking.

After a moment, Jermyn followed her, wrestling with what he'd heard. *I thought Lady Jean stopped working magic because she was old. I wonder if Master Eschar knows? It doesn't seem fair to Brianne.*

She shouldn't have to study with a hedgewitch. That could be as dangerous as—as whatever her mother was doing.

He was surprised, a little. *You'd think Mistress Allons would know that you can't block talent and desire. Besides, magical accidents are rare—sorcery's no more risky a profession than a lot of others. And if Brianne really has the talent. . . .* That, of course, was the major sticking point: whether or not Brianne really had the talent.

"Would you like me to talk to Master Eschar?" he offered finally. "He's good at solving problems. Maybe he could convince your grandmother to—to do something."

Wearily, she shook her head. "No one can convince Gran to change her mind once it's made up. Believe me, I know. She'll just tell me to be patient, like she always does—as if Father will suddenly change his mind one day. That's as bad as Uncle Eben saying I'm too young. Besides, your Master Eschar isn't going to be around very long. Gran said this afternoon that she has to give the party by the day after tomorrow because he'll probably be leaving the day after that."

"What party?" They had reached Tower Landing; Brianne led the way to a side door.

"Gran's giving a tea party so the neighbors can meet Master Eschar and you," she said, sighing. "A *formal* high tea, with everyone invited. Father says we haven't had one of those since before I was born. It's going to be an awful lot of work, which is why I had to come to Maudie today. I won't have time later. I just wish—oh, I don't know what I wish. It's mostly for Master Eschar, anyway, because he's the Theoretician and so famous. I think she's going to tell everyone about it tonight at dinner."

Dinner? Delia said eagerly from his shoulder. She sounded hungry. *Dinner now?*

"My dinner, not yours," he told her firmly, starting up the stairs. "*You* will stay in the bedroom until I get back to feed you."

"It's awfully confusing when you talk to her like that," Brianne said from where she'd stopped at the foot of the stairs. "I only get to hear half the conversation."

Jermyn shrugged. "You'll get used to it. I've listened to my aunt talk to her familiar all my life. . . ."

His voice trailed off. Brianne was certainly old enough to attract a familiar, if she was a wizard. Unless she was a spellmaker, of course—spellmakers tended to be older. *Like me,* he thought. *I was even older than Brianne is now when I got Dee.* And how worried he'd been about maybe not having any talent. He still didn't like to remember those days. But if Lady Jean said that Brianne wasn't a spellmaker, then she probably wasn't. Was the fact that she *didn't* already have a familiar a sign that she had no talent for other types of sorcery?

Brianne was looking up at him with a carefully blank face. "Are you going to tell on me?" she said, twisting her hands in the front of her cloak.

He paused on the landing, looking back. "I don't know," he answered honestly. "I just don't know what I should do."

3

TEA PARTY

TWO DAYS LATER, he still hadn't decided. There just didn't seem to be any comfortable answer. Even asking Master Eschar what to do didn't feel right.

The Theoretician spent most of his time buried in the library, crooning over Lady Jean's collection of rare books and manuscripts. Lady Jean joined him occasionally, but seldom for long; she seemed to spend her days in her workroom. And Brianne herself was busy supervising preparations for the party. Every time Jermyn tried to approach her she had to rush off to deal with some crisis or other.

If only he could get her to talk—or at least to

notice him. Maybe together they could come up with a plan.

The only good thing that happened was that he and Delia discovered Lady Jean's conservatory, which was large, green, and fragrant with the most enticing odors. Delia was fascinated. Phineas, the coachman and man-of-all-work, had been dubious about Delia until Jermyn assured him that the skunk never sprayed indoors. Then he'd agreed to let her explore.

Delia does like the plants, Jermyn thought as he was getting ready for Lady Jean's party. *That's good. I can take her in there to exercise when the weather gets really cold.* "Won't that be nice, Dee?"

Uh-huh, she said agreeably, from her position curled up on his pillow. *Go for walk?*

"You know I can't," he told her, pulling his best tunic straight. "I have to go to the tea party. And *wasn't* Master Eschar annoyed when he heard about it! You know how he hates big parties, but Mistress Allons didn't give him a chance to say no."

Delia cocked her head at him. *Quiet*, she said. It was her way of telling him that she was bored.

"Well, I can't do anything about it right now," he said, frowning. "You've got to stay out of the way. We can't risk having the guests see you."

She put her nose between her front paws, sulking. Delia didn't like being hustled out of the way as if she were an embarrassment. *Huh.*

"Yes, I know you're insulted, but it can't be helped," he told her firmly. "At least the staff is getting used to you. None of the maids has screamed or dropped anything since yesterday, and I think old Phineas could get to like you. He was interested when I told him how much you like to chase rats."

She lifted her head alertly. *Rats?*

"Yes, rats. He says they've been sneaking into the conservatory, with the cold weather coming on, and Mistress Allons won't allow a cat indoors." That was another part of the puzzle that Jermyn couldn't fit together; even if she didn't want a familiar, why not have a cat around the house to keep the mice and rats down? "Be good, and you can go rat hunting."

Good Je'm'n, she said, and minced across the bedclothes to sniff at him. *All pretty-clean.*

He grinned at her. "Thank you. Promise to stay out of sight, and I won't lock you in. All right?"

Promise, she said, and plopped off of the bed to the floor. *Go look window.*

He left her sitting by the window, her nose pressed to the cold glass. It was snowing outside again, but not too heavily; Duncan Campbell said that the guests would have no difficulty getting through.

On the way downstairs, Jermyn's frown returned. Brianne's father was the biggest part of her problem, Jermyn thought, settling his collar. *I don't blame him for not liking magic, but he's wrong. If Brianne really has magical ability, it will be more dangerous for her not to train than to study in the Guild.*

Firmly, he put the thought out of his head. This was no time to worry. The receiving line was set up in the small front parlor; through the doors Jermyn could see the long parlor, which opened on the conservatory. Lady Jean was already seated near the fire, with Master Eschar and her son-in-law standing beside her. Jermyn took his place next to Duncan.

"Where's Brianne?" he asked, looking around the room.

"She's behind the tea table," her father said shortly. "Serving."

"Oh. Right. Of course."

Lady Jean was already greeting her first guests, an older couple. "I'm so pleased you could come," she was saying. "William, you remember the Kestrells?"

Master Eschar shook hands with real warmth. "Yes, of course I remember Alex and Matilde. And how is little Jemima?"

Mr. Kestrell chuckled. "Not so little anymore. She's a journeyman healer now—sends her regrets, I'm afraid."

"She did say she'd try to drop in later, if she could," Mrs. Kestrell put in. "You understand how it is with healers."

"Yes, of course," Master Eschar said. "Always on call."

Mr. Kestrell stayed to chat with Lady Jean and Master Eschar, but his wife moved down the line. A small ruffled pigeon of a woman, she reminded Jermyn of his aunt.

"Hello, Duncan," she said, holding out her hand. "Jemima sends her best wishes, as I'm sure you know—to you and Brianne, especially."

"Thank you, Matilde," he said stiffly. "My best to her, as well. I don't believe you've met Jermyn Graves, Mother's new student."

"Hello, Jermyn," she said, smiling. "How do you like Land's End?"

"Well, I haven't seen much of it yet," he said, temporizing. "I expect I'll like it fine, especially after I meet some people."

"I hope so," she told him. She hesitated, glancing at Duncan as if trying to decide what she should say next. "I'd heard—that is, word in the village is that *everyone* will be here today."

"I believe so," Duncan said, even more stiffly. He looked over toward his mother-in-law—warningly, Jermyn thought. "*Everyone* was invited."

Now, what is that about? "Brianne worked awfully hard, getting ready for it," Jermyn said.

Mrs. Kestrell tilted her head sideways. "Duncan, you didn't ask that child to run this whole affair by herself, did you? You did. Shame on you."

He bristled. "Brianne is perfectly capable—"

"Yes, yes, I know, but she *is* just fourteen, and of course Jean has never—why on earth didn't you ask for help? I would have been glad to come to the Tower for a few days. Or Jemima, if she could have managed it. Really, Duncan, you should have known better."

She talks to him as if he's younger than I am, Jermyn thought, amused. *And he doesn't like it one bit.*

Then the line started moving again. Mrs. Kestrell left, looking annoyed. Her husband shook hands with Duncan and Jermyn before joining her in the main room. Two elderly couples crowded in next, then a group of younger people. After that, Jermyn lost track. There was a great deal of noise and bustle, and he found himself shaking hands without even trying to catch the names. *I suppose I'll meet the important ones again later,* he consoled himself. *Or I can ask Master Eschar who was who.*

Finally the stream of guests slowed. Jermyn had just started to hope that everyone had arrived when another older couple entered. He was short and round and she was tall and wide; both were dressed more expensively than anyone else in the room, including Lady Jean.

The woman greeted Lady Jean with a little cry of joy. "Jean, *darling!* It's been *far* too long."

Mistress Allons answered her calmly. "Reginald,

44

Lydia, so good of you to come. William, you remember Lord and Lady Poncebry, don't you? They are my very good neighbors to the south."

The way she said it made Jermyn think that Master Eschar had *better* remember them, if he knew what was good for him. Evidently, the Theoretician agreed.

"Of course I do," he said, with false heartiness.

"We had some good times in the old days, with you and the other students, hah?" the man said, shaking Eschar's hand. "Good hunting."

"Hunting—oh, yes, you used to take us hunting," Eschar said, as if a light had just dawned. Jermyn bit back a smile.

"I'd take you out again, if you were going to be around long enough," Lord Poncebry told him. "We've got vermin all through the home farm, and I wouldn't say no to an opportunity to clean 'em out. Right, Duncan? . . . Who's this? The apprentice? Well, we'd have him along, too—more the merrier."

"Now, Reginald, don't you start," Lady Poncebry said, shaking a finger at him. "We've much more important things to talk about than your old hunting. Tell me, Master Eschar, what news from Court?"

"Not a great deal, I'm afraid," Eschar said, his eyes glazing slightly. "I'm semiretired, these days, and I rarely attend Court functions."

"Oh, but you can tell me what the ladies have been wearing." She tittered. "One does so miss the intimate little details, living as far from the Court as we do. If I have told Reginald once, I have told him a thousand times—Reginald, I say, we must have a season in the city. Surely—"

She ran on like water flowing, trying to ask about fashions and gossip until Jermyn had to fight to hold in his laughter. As if the Master Theoretician ever paid any attention to whether heeled shoes or double-tiered skirts were going in or out of style! Finally, Lady Jean put a stop to it.

"I'm sure that William would be happy to discuss Court fashions with you at length, Lydia," she said firmly, "later."

"You know more than I do, then," Eschar said softly, as Lord and Lady Poncebry left the line.

"Behave yourself." The party seemed to have enlivened Lady Jean. She held herself as straight as ever and her tone was still admonishing, but there was a lurking spark in her eyes that Jermyn hadn't noticed before. It gave him hope—almost.

"Yes, ma'am," Eschar said obediently, as repentant as a small child caught with his hand in the cookie jar. He caught Jermyn's eye and grinned. "*Lovely* party, isn't it, Jermyn."

"Yes, sir," Jermyn said temperately, not responding to his apprentice-master's sarcasm. It didn't seem like a good idea with Lady Jean right there.

Whatever Lady Jean might have said was cut off by a new arrival.

"Hello, Mother, Duncan," said a tall man from the doorway. He shook off his damp cloak and handed it to Phineas. "How is Brianne? William, it's been a long time."

"Good afternoon, Eben," Jean said, her voice and face suddenly frozen.

Jermyn looked at the man curiously. "Uncle Eben," Brianne had said. *He's got to be Lady Jean's son, the Priest. Powers, but she certainly doesn't sound very happy to see him.*

Eben Allons had curly ginger hair, only slightly gray, and his mother's vivid blue eyes. He seemed to be about Master Eschar's age, though his broad, open face made him look younger. Jermyn liked him on sight.

"My granddaughter is quite well, thank you," Lady Jean said as if talking to a stranger. "Duncan, it would seem that there are no more guests to arrive."

"Yes, of course, Mother," he said, glancing apologetically at his brother-in-law. "Shall we go in?"

He offered her his arm, and she took it, standing slowly. "Yes. Tea would be very good now, I believe. William, remember—you are guest of honor and must circulate to be polite."

She didn't glance at Eben as she spoke; he might not have been there.

"Yes, ma'am," Eschar said, looking surprised and worried as he watched her walk into the main parlor. Then he turned back to Eben, his expression clearing. "Hello yourself, Eben. It *has* been a long time. How is life in the village these days? Does the Church still suit you as well as it did the last time we talked?"

"Yes, for the most part," Eben said. He was looking after his mother, his mouth set. "Except for—certain inevitable difficulties."

"So I see," Eschar said, frowning. "Well—first things first. Jermyn, let me introduce you to Eben Allons."

"Hello," Jermyn said, offering his hand. "It's nice to meet you."

"And yourself, Jermyn," Eben said. "I suppose everybody calls you Jerry—no? Jermyn it is, then. I've been looking forward to embarrassing William here with tales about our student days."

"Really?" Jermyn said, interested.

"Oh, Jermyn knows all my faults," the Theoretician said. "You can't shock him. But, Eben"— his voice lowered—"I hadn't realized—is the rift still so deep between you and Jean? After all these years. . . ."

Eben sighed, running one hand through curly hair. "It's been worse, I suppose. Right after my sister died, perhaps . . . however, it's bad enough. Mother doesn't change, William, and I've given up hoping. If she had her way, I would have ceased to exist when I defied her and entered the Church. Since I'm the village priest now, she has to invite me to social events like this one—which is probably why she has so few parties. If only she'd let me transfer. I've requested a city parish often enough, but the Lady of the Manor keeps blocking my departure."

He sounded so bitter that Jermyn blinked. Master Eschar looked taken aback. "Surely it isn't *that* bad—"

"In some ways, it's worse than you can imagine," Eben said, his blue eyes distant. "Mother hasn't been the same since—my poor Annalise. Even through the worst of things, *she* made us a family. Without her, we have very little to say to each other, but Mother still won't let go."

That must have been what Mrs. Kestrell was thinking of when she asked if everyone was invited, Jermyn realized. *The whole village must know that Lady Jean and her son don't get along.*

"Was Annalise Brianne's mother?" Jermyn asked. At least, it figured that that was her name. He picked up a warning glance from Eschar, but it was too late to take the words back.

"Yes, my sister, Annalise," Eben said, then stopped. He shot a rueful glance at Master Eschar. "You sound almost as if you didn't know—William, didn't you tell this boy the whole terrible story?"

The Theoretician looked uncomfortable. "I told

him what was relevant. I did think—that is, we had so little time for personal matters . . . or ancient history."

Eben snorted. "You mean that, as usual, you couldn't bring yourself to gossip. William, in this house ancient history is far more important than current events."

"I do know some things," Jermyn put in hastily; he didn't like seeing Master Eschar made uncomfortable. "Master Eschar told me about the accident, and Brianne said that that's why her father—hates magic."

He managed to catch himself before saying *that's why her father won't let her study magic;* it didn't seem wise to turn the conversation that way just yet.

"I knew you were in the Church, too," he added. "But no one said anything about you being—about Mistress Allons being upset with you. Not even Brianne."

"Brianne wouldn't," Eben said, sighing. The bitterness seemed to drain out of him. "Poor child—she's too often caught in the middle. Of course she feels she must support her grandmother, but she's fond of me, you see."

"I still don't understand why it's so bad between you and Jean," Eschar said, troubled. "She was never so unreasonable. Perhaps if I spoke to her. . . ."

"Let it go, William," Eben said softly. "Do what you came to do, and then leave—don't try to help. Do you think others haven't tried? No doubt I am as much to blame as Mother, but I find that I don't want her charity."

"I—understand," Eschar said, sounding unhappy. "I'm sorry."

Eben shrugged. "I've learned to live with it. Duncan and I get along fairly well, when Mother isn't around. And Brianne is a dear child."

Still talking, they walked into the room. Jermyn followed, thinking furiously. *So that's Brianne's uncle. He seems more sensible than her father, anyway. Or her grandmother. How could Lady Jean disown her son just because he wanted to be a priest?* He tried to imagine doing something so terrible that Aunt Merry would disown him, and he had to give up. She might be furious, she might even be ashamed and disappointed, but he didn't believe that she would ever deny him. *Well, maybe if I murdered somebody.*

The long parlor was sparkling with light and noise, the inner wall dominated by a second great hearth set off by a veined marble mantel. Master Eschar had said that the portrait over it, of a stern man with impressive mustaches, was Lady Jean's father. On the opposite wall was a portrait of Lady Jean herself as a young woman. Except for the red-gold hair tied back in a severe knot, she looked almost the same.

Brianne and the tea table stood at the end of the parlor, just across from the double glass doors to the conservatory. She was wearing a soft blue dress that laced up the front, with full sleeves. Jermyn liked the way the dress brought out the color of her eyes, but he couldn't figure out how to say so without sounding silly. *She looks awfully pretty in that dress*, he thought. *Not beautiful, but—awfully pretty.*

"Nice party," he ventured, accepting a cup of tea and a watercress sandwich. For some reason, he felt shy, maybe because she hadn't said ten words to him since they'd come back from Maudie's. Or maybe because he'd been talking about her with her uncle and she didn't know it.

"Thank you," she said primly, pushing a loose strand of hair back over her ear and not meeting his eyes. "Did everyone get through the snow all right?"

"I think so," he told her. "I just met your uncle."

She looked up. "Is Uncle Eben here? Oh, I'm so glad—that is, I didn't see him come in."

"He's over by the window, talking to Master Eschar," Jermyn said. "Brianne, why didn't you tell me about—"

"What? I'm sorry, Jermyn," she said, exactly as she had every time he'd tried to talk to her since they'd gotten back from the woods. "I've got to check the cream cakes. Cook wasn't sure there would be enough of them."

Moving swiftly, she disappeared into the animated crowd. Jermyn bit his lip in frustration. True, a formal tea party wasn't any place for serious discussion, but did she have to run away from him like that? *Well, I'll just stand here until she gets back,* he thought, biting into his sandwich.

He'd finished the sandwich and a second cup of tea, with no sign of Brianne, when he began to realize that something was wrong. There was something in the air—like the elusive odor of dried flowers, like a musical scale just slightly out of tune. . . .

Magic.

Startled, he looked for Lady Jean. She was sitting by the fire, talking to Mrs. Kestrell, so it wasn't her. She didn't even seem to notice the smell of magic. *And I know it isn't me,* he thought. *But who?*

He turned to the wall, ostensibly to study a summer landscape hanging behind the tea table. Half closing his eyes, he extended his senses. Nothing. Nothing but the golden rope of the familiar-link connecting him to Delia. Though it was quiet when he wasn't pulling power through it, the link was always, comfortingly, there.

Je'm'n? Delia asked, surprised. *Je'm'n, here?*

There's someone working magic in the room,

Dee, he thought at her in frustration. *Or at least, there's some magic—and I don't like it.*

Which was the simple truth, he realized as he framed the words. Whatever the faint trace was, it made his stomach roll slightly.

Huh. He sensed Delia focusing, letting him use her senses as well as his own, but she was too far away to do him much good that way. Realizing it instinctively—she was very good at figuring out what he needed—she sent him a vision of herself slipping through the conservatory, a dark shadow in all the leafy green. *Yes-yes?*

Well . . . all right, he thought at her. *If you can get to the conservatory without anyone seeing you, come on. Maybe together we'll be able to trace this magic back. Only hide, you hear me? Hide deep in the bushes.*

Unobtrusively, he scanned the room. The conservatory doors were open, for those guests who were interested in hothouse flowers, but Delia shouldn't have any problems concealing herself in all that shrubbery. Moving away from the tea table to a place where he could lean against the wall, he waited.

Here, Je'm'n, his familiar said in a few minutes. *All safe.*

From a bush to one side of the glass conservatory doors poked a small black nose.

Good, he said. *Here we go.*

He reached cautiously out along the familiar-link, searching. There was the hint of power he'd noticed before, looking even darker and more shadowy in the light of his own wizardry. Cautiously, he started to follow it back, looking for the source.

In the back of his mind, Delia hissed. *Careful, Je'm'n!*

The spell twisted away from him as he tried to hang on to it. Grimly, he picked up the strand and traced it. *Here—no, that way. What a tangled mess.*

Then, as suddenly as if a door had been slammed shut, it was gone. Jermyn choked and would have staggered if he hadn't been leaning against the wall. Delia sent him a mental chitter of dismay; she was as surprised as he was. *Did you see that?* he thought to her. *But magic shouldn't just disappear completely. There ought to be a remnant at least, a fragment of broken spell or something—where did it go?*

She didn't have an answer. Neither did he—but one occurred to him when he looked over at the tea table and saw Brianne with a tray of cakes.

Brianne and her lessons. *Could this be* her *doing?* he thought, frowning. *If so, I will have to tell on her, right now. I didn't like the feel of that magic at all.*

He stepped over to the table. "We need to talk," he said.

"Oh—Jermyn," she said, setting down the tray. "I was just getting some fresh cream cakes from the kitchen. Do you think we need more sandwiches?" She sounded flustered.

"I don't know and I don't care," he said, taking her by the elbow and steering her over to one side.

"Well, I *have* to care," she said, with some asperity. "Look, I'm too busy to talk right now—"

"Are you too busy to work magic?" he asked.

"What do you mean?" she said, glancing anxiously around the room.

He groaned. "I knew it. You've been using something you learned from Maudie, haven't you, and it's gone wrong."

"I didn't learn it from Maudie, exactly, and I don't think it's gone wrong," she said guiltily. "It was just one of the regular kitchen spells, the one against spoilage in the preserve cupboard. I—um—I used it on the cream cakes, because Cook had to make them yesterday and I was afraid they'd go stale. I—I only rewrote the pentangle so that it was wider than usual . . . not too much, just enough to take in the whole pantry along with the cupboard. That's all right, isn't it? I know I wasn't supposed to, but the description of the spell said it was possible for special occasions. . . ."

That can't be it. Jermyn frowned. *Well, maybe it can.* "Are you sure that's all you did?"

56

"Yes, that's all," she said. "I was afraid Cook would notice if I tried anything more. Anyway, why are you so worried? I did it yesterday—it should have faded by now. I erased the chalk marks in the pantry first thing this morning."

Jermyn opened his mouth to explain, but before he could say anything a shrill scream from the conservatory cut through the sustained hum of conversation in the parlor.

Delia, I told you to hide! Jermyn said, jumping to the logical conclusion.

Did hide, she answered indignantly. *Rats in the bushes—run away—*

He received a hasty image of shadows scurrying frantically across the conservatory floor and right under a woman's skirts. But if someone saw a frightened rat, then someone else might easily look to see what the rat was running from.

Je'm'n! his familiar squealed, before he could finish the thought. She sounded almost panicky. *Je'm'n come quick!*

He ran. Just inside the glass doors of the conservatory, Lydia Poncebry was standing on a walkway next to an overturned orchid, with her hands pressed to her cheeks and her eyes wide with horror.

"Get it! Get it! Get it!" she yelped, backing away. Her voice rose and fell in ear-piercing waves.

"Filthy beast!" her husband shouted. He was

swatting at a nearby fig tree with the broken end of a narrow board. Beneath the greenery, Jermyn glimpsed a black-and-white shape scurrying for cover.

"Stop that!" he yelled at Reginald. Delia wouldn't spray indoors, and she obviously hadn't been startled into misbehaving—but her obedience left her without any real defense. "Stop that right now!"

His fingers laced and he reached along the familiar-link to Delia to pull magic into himself. She greeted him with a little grunt of relief as the rainbow of colors started to flicker from his hands. The shield spell had been one of the first Aunt Merry had taught him, and it was still one of the ones that he did best—all he had to do was shift the energy *here* and *there* to use it offensively. As the arc of color spread out in front of him to envelop Reginald Poncebry in its confining folds, Jermyn felt a rush of satisfaction. *There, you. Attack my familiar, will you? She wasn't doing you any harm.*

"What—what—who—" Reginald dropped the board and tried to turn to face this new threat, but Jermyn's spell locked him firmly into place.

"I said, *stop*," Jermyn said, reinforcing the command with a rush of magic. "Delia won't hurt you."

"You—you brute!" Lydia sobbed. She rushed at Jermyn and started to beat against his back with her fists. Hastily, he included her in the shield-spell. "Leave him alone, you vicious—oh!"

The spell caught her too, and it held her like a statue next to her husband. Delia poked her nose out of the plants and hissed. *Je'm'n! Hurt? She hit —bad!*

"No, of course I'm not hurt," he said, breathing a little rapidly. He dropped to one knee and scooped her into his arms. "She can't hit that hard. Are *you* all right?"

Bad man. She squirmed in his grasp to hiss again, at Reginald. *Rats run out, then silly screamer and bad man with stick come. Make fuss—in house!*

"They certainly did," he said, glaring at the Poncebrys. "But don't worry, I won't let them—"

"What is going on here?" Lady Jean said from behind him. Her voice was blizzard cold. "Mr. Graves?"

He whirled, Delia still clutched tightly against his chest. Mistress Allons was standing in the doorway, with a wide-eyed Brianne on one side and Master Eschar on the other. Behind them crowded most of the guests.

"I—I—that is, we—" Jermyn stuttered, looking wildly from the door to his magic-held victims. Delia whimpered and nuzzled under his chin with her cold nose. "I didn't think—"

"So much is obvious," she said in freezing disapproval.

The tea party was most definitely over.

4

CONSEQUENCES

MASTER ESCHAR'S reaction didn't help at all, Jermyn thought resentfully. The Theoretician managed to contain his laughter until after the guests had departed, but not an instant longer. Then he howled.

Mistress Allons was not amused.

"I hold you at least partially responsible for this—this disaster," she told Eschar tightly, when he finally stopped chuckling. "Clearly you have been remiss in disciplining your apprentice."

"I've no doubt I have," he said, wiping his eyes with a large white kerchief. "However, when you've known Jermyn's Delia as long as I have, you will doubtless come to understand that sometimes there is nothing one can do *but* laugh. At length. I could tell you stories. . . ."

He showed signs of breaking down again.

"Please do not," Lady Jean said icily. She turned to Jermyn, who, with Delia bristling protectively at his feet, had been picking up the spilled orchid. "Mr. Graves, you will finish cleaning up this mess, and then wait outside my study door until I am ready to speak to you. I suggest you and your familiar occupy yourselves with contemplating what might be the consequences of such behavior."

"Yes, ma'am," Jermyn said dismally. He glanced at Master Eschar for reassurance, but the Theoretician had stopped laughing. He was looking at Lady Jean with a disturbed expression.

Her voice became even colder. "That will be all."

Waiting on the long wooden bench outside Lady Jean's study for what seemed like hours, Jermyn sat with his back straight and his hands clenched at his sides. The study was in the tower, near his own rooms. She could as easily have told him to wait in his own workroom until she was ready to see him. The humiliation of sitting in the hall like a naughty boy at dame school was obviously intended to remind him of his place.

Not that it bothered him. Much.

What she was likely to say about Delia did bother him, a great deal.

It's not fair, he thought, trying to keep his thoughts private so he wouldn't disturb Delia. *Dee did everything right. She hid, just like I told her to. It wasn't her fault the rats were frightened of her. This is her home now. She ought be able to poke around in it without some stupid lord-person trying to kill her.*

Uneasily, he was aware that he shouldn't have told her to come to him, especially since his plan hadn't succeeded. He still didn't know who had been working magic at Lady Jean's tea party. It wasn't Brianne, not if she was telling the truth . . . and he thought she was. But who else could it have been? Unless he'd been imagining things.

Cuddled tightly beside him, Delia nuzzled one fist. *Je'm'n? Sorry-sorry, Je'm'n.*

He might have known he couldn't hide what he was feeling from her; the bond between them was too close. But her tone made him even more angry. She hadn't sounded so remorseful since she was a confused and clumsy kit, trying desperately to figure out what he wanted her to do. Convulsively, he gathered her into his lap and squeezed.

"It *isn't* your fault," he whispered to her fiercely. *You live here, just like I do—you live wherever I* live, she must know that. You should have the same rights as anyone at Tower Landing.

He buried his face in Delia's neck. *Maybe Lady Jean won't want me anymore. Maybe I'll have to go back to the city with Master Eschar.*

He wasn't sure if that idea made him unhappy or not. He hadn't had much time to be homesick since the sea voyage, but now he thought of Aunt Merry and the cozy little shop on Thornapple Lane—and Master Eschar's elegant, book-filled house across town on Wisteria Street—with a fierce longing. He had a place there, people who knew him and trusted him. So what if he couldn't study with *the* Spellmaker? He could work with the Healers' Guild instead. Healers were earth wizards, too, like spellmakers, if of a different order. They could train him if they had to. Master Eschar had told him so when he'd worried about how old Lady Jean was and how she might die before Jermyn was ready to go to her. It wouldn't be easy, but he could—

No, I couldn't, he thought, sighing. *So long as there is a Master Spellmaker, the Guild will expect me to study with her. If I can't, then I can't be a journeyman spellmaker. Period. The Healers' Guild is just a poor substitute. Otherwise, all the candidates that Lady Jean has turned down over the years would have tried to do it that way. I'm lucky she accepted me, and she probably wouldn't have if Master Eschar hadn't spoken for me.*

Delia squirmed in his arms, gratified but made uncomfortable by his show of affection. She arched her back. *Je'm'n better now?*

"Hmm? Oh, sorry, Dee." He set her down on the bench, where she sat up and looked at him with warm black eyes. *If Mistress Allons had a familiar, or even a pet, she'd understand how I felt when I saw Lord Poncebry whacking away with that board. She must have had a familiar once. Why doesn't she now? Maybe if I ask, she'll explain. And then I can explain.* "Yes, I'm better now. It wasn't your fault."

No. She rested her chin on his leg. *Rats all run away. Silly screamer and bad man make noisy-messy.*

The door opened behind him. Hastily, he got to his feet.

"Come in," said Lady Jean's voice.

Swallowing, he obeyed.

Mistress Allons's workroom was a large round area with a central hearth for heating. There was a fire in the hearth, the white ash on the big logs showing that it had been burning for some time. The walls curved gently; they were covered floor to ceiling with shelving filled with books and glass cases. At one side of the great room was a free-standing circular table with a velvet-wrapped bundle in the center. Jermyn knew what that must be— Lady Jean's crystal. Wistfully, he wondered if she would ever let him use it to talk to Aunt Merry.

Opposite the table was a desk covered with papers piled in rough stacks. Windows lined two of the walls, great triple-arched openings each centered in a deep niche and facing south and east respectively. In one niche, a second, smaller desk sat on a thick embroidered carpet, with a painter's easel tilted next to it so as to catch the light from the window. Jermyn had to turn his head slightly to see the painting: It was a half-finished portrait of a woman who looked startlingly like an older version of Brianne. *That must be Annalise, the daughter*, he thought. *I guess Brianne takes after her mother*. The paints were cracked with age, and he wondered uneasily how long the picture had been on the easel. The other niche was filled with a small, shabby sofa. On one side of the circular hearth, matching stuffed chairs were grouped around a low table. It was all spotlessly clean, if disorganized, and it would have looked very comfortable and welcoming to Jermyn if it were not for the woman standing next to the hearth.

Effortlessly, Lady Jean dominated the great room. She was still wearing the amber silk dress that she had put on for the tea party, but she'd thrown a white lace shawl around her shoulders. It did not make her look any less forbidding. "Come in, Mr. Graves," she said. "Sit down."

Hesitantly, Jermyn sat in one of the two easy chairs as Lady Jean sank into the one opposite. He settled Delia on his lap.

"No." Lady Jean pointed to an embroidered footstool that he hadn't noticed before. "The animal will sit there."

Jermyn opened his mouth to protest, but he closed it when Delia grudgingly crawled down from his lap and obediently hauled herself up onto the footstool. *Dee? You don't mind?*

Lady said, she grumbled, showing him an image of Mistress Allons. The intimacy of her tone indicated that she hadn't just heard Lady Jean's spoken words; she'd sensed the command mentally.

"You—you can talk to *my* familiar!" Jermyn started the sentence as a question but it came out like an accusation. He'd sometimes been able to understand what Aunt Merry's cat, Pol, was saying, deducing the meaning from action or expression, but no one ought to be able to talk directly to a wizard's familiar but the wizard himself.

The Spellmaker was neither annoyed nor surprised at his words—or at his half-hidden resentment. Impassively, she nodded. "Yes. I can make myself understood to most familiars well enough. You will find that there are many odd and individual abilities that go with being a spellmaker. Magic has strange corners."

Jermyn caught himself just before he complained and made a complete fool of himself. Again. Instead, he asked, "Why can't I hear other wizards' familiars?"

"Have you ever really tried?" she asked him.

"No." He thought again and shook his head. "No, not really."

"Sorcery offers but it does not give, young man," she said, sitting up very straight, hands folded in her lap. "You must work to earn its favors. And that, after all, is what we are here to discuss."

The apparent change of subject confused Jermyn. On her stool, Delia shifted uneasily. "I thought we were going to talk about—about what happened in the conservatory."

"What happened in the conservatory is a symptom of the disease, not the disease itself." Her vivid blue eyes looked at him levelly. "You used magic on a guest in this house—on two guests, both without magical abilities of their own. Am I correct?"

"Well—yes. But—"

She lifted one thin hand to cut him off. "No excuses. No explanation can possibly help. You essentially shaped a spell and threw it, in a fit of temper. What if the spell had gone awry? What if, instead of trapping your victims, the spell had closed on them and continued to close?"

He could feel himself going pale. Delia whimpered and nudged his knee. Automatically, he stroked her narrow head. "It never has before when I've used a shield spell."

"Perhaps not," she said. "But the circumstances weren't exactly the same this time, were they? You weren't just invoking a familiar magical structure. You were changing it, recreating it to suit the circumstances. In other words, this was a new spell, one you made in the moment, without testing and with no safeguards. Could you create it again, here and now, and be sure of getting the same effect?"

"N-no." He didn't *think* he could. Not exactly.

"Then you cannot be certain of its potential," she told him, her eyes staring straight through him. "Can you?"

"No." Jermyn bit his lower lip. When Lady Jean had talked about consequences, he'd assumed she meant selecting an appropriate punishment—not *this*. "I—I guess I didn't think. I'm sorry."

Mistress Allons leaned back, her shoulders untensing slightly. "Being sorry would not have helped my guests if you had strangled or suffocated them. I doubt I could have solved your spell in time to save them, and William has no practical magic. We might easily have had a double funeral on our hands."

But we didn't, he wanted to say. *Doesn't that count for something?*

Not for much, it seemed. Lady Jean turned to look into the heart of the fire.

"Magic is a burden," she mused, talking as much to herself as to him. "All power is responsibility, but magic more than most. And the power of the spellmaker, above all others, requires *discipline*."

"Yes, ma'am," he managed to say, wondering if she were thinking about her daughter. "Does this mean you won't accept me as your journeyman?"

She looked at him sharply. "I have already accepted you as my journeyman."

He was so relieved that he almost forgot to be confused. "But—you don't think I have enough discipline—"

"That is not entirely your doing," she said, at her most regal. He flushed; if she criticized Master Eschar or Aunt Merry, then he *would* give her a sharp answer, Master Spellmaker or not. Instead, she smiled, surprising him again. "What this unfortunate incident means, young man, is that you are going to work very hard over the next few months. You will obey my orders before your own desires and needs, you and your familiar both. That your familiar is unusual and requires special living conditions is of no importance. We will settle such matters as time goes on. *You* will work no magic, with her or without her, unless at my express command. If you want to scratch an itch on your nose while outlining a spell, I expect you to ask permission. Until I say otherwise. Is that clear?"

"Yes, ma'am," he said, nodding vigorously. "I swear."

Her smile grew broader, and he looked at it uneasily. Delia whimpered again, almost inaudibly.

"You have already sworn, young Jermyn. When you entered the Guild, you gave oath to abide by the laws and customs of the Guild. You are not a hedgewitch, like poor Maudlin Mattock—yes, of course I know about our local hedgewitch," she said impatiently, when he twitched in involuntary response. "So should you, by now—she lives close enough to the Tower. In fact, I've felt you puzzling over something, and I assumed you'd sensed her presence in the woods. Haven't you?"

"I guess so. . . ." Had that been what he'd sensed at the tea party, after all? Just the hedgewitch, doing some hedgewitchery in her hut? *I did think of Maudie at first*, he remembered. *It seemed closer, though. Actually in the tower, but—well, maybe she was closer. Only, why didn't Delia recognize Maudie's magic, even if I didn't?* "I—I wasn't sure what it was, exactly. I guess it could have been a hedgewitch. . . ."

Lady Jean nodded. "As I thought. But you needn't worry about Maudlin. The Guild judged and dismissed her long ago, when she was almost as young as you are now. Policy in country districts is to leave the local 'wisewoman' in place, you know, unless she is actively malicious—which our Maudlin is not, I assure you."

"I didn't realize that was Guild policy," he said slowly. *She knows about Maudie. Does that mean she knows about Brianne's lessons, too? And if she does know, then does she approve?* "No one pays much attention to hedgewitches in the city."

"Or in the country, for the most part. Maudlin is no longer any concern of the Guild's," Lady Jean said, dismissing the subject. "You, on the other hand, are a Guild wizard, bound to its discipline. As your journeyman-master, I have the authority of the Guild, of Imperial law, and of the Powers Themselves behind me. If you have it in you, I will make you a spellmaker. If not—well, we will find it out soon enough."

When at last he closed the door behind him, Jermyn was as tired as if he'd been working a Great Magic. The feeling that he'd behaved irresponsibly was the worst—far worse than any punishment could be.

The actual punishment itself wasn't too bad. He was confined to Tower Landing for the next several days, and Delia was not to go off the grounds. She was also forbidden to visit the conservatory alone, but Lady Jean had graciously given her permission to hunt rats there, provided that either Jermyn or Phineas the coachman were with her. In addition, Jermyn's weekly schedule had several hours of physical labor added to it, including chopping wood and maintaining the fire in Lady Jean's workroom. All in all, it was better than he'd expected.

But Lady Jean's attitude—her stern coldness toward him—had left him numb and shaking, so that he'd had to fight to keep his hands steady when he picked up Delia to leave. He hadn't been able to ask Lady Jean about his studies, or about why she didn't have a familiar of her own or at least a cat for the rats. He was beginning to think that he would never dare ask her anything.

"Not being able to ask any questions is going to make studying with her an interesting experience, though," he muttered to the empty air of the hallway. *If only she didn't make me feel like such a grubby little boy. . . .*

Delia nuzzled his chin. *Out?*

"What? Oh—" She sent him a picture of Master Eschar standing on the west terrace with his pipe in his hand. Lady Jean didn't like the odor of smoke in the house. "Yes, I think I would like to talk to Master Eschar. How did you know that? For that matter, how did you know he wasn't in his room?"

She sniffed at him. *Smell. Go talk-talk out—come too?*

Of course she would have been able to scent the Theoretician's presence or absence on this floor—his room was right next to Jermyn's. And she probably also sensed Jermyn's need to talk to someone. "I can't hide things from you, can I? Sure, you can come. *Master Eschar* likes you. Let me get my heavy cloak."

72

They found the Theoretician leaning against the stone railing, looking out into the snow-covered cloister. Delia squeaked happily at the shadows. When Jermyn nodded his permission, she dashed out to explore the evergreen bushes.

Master Eschar nodded. "Hello, Jermyn. Bloody but unbowed, I see."

"I suppose." Jermyn moodily kicked at a clump of snow. "Master, I didn't mean to risk harming those two in the conservatory. But Delia wouldn't spray indoors, and I was afraid Lord Poncebry would hurt her."

"I know," Eschar said, puffing smoke. "Jean said that your familiar showed admirable discipline and training."

"She did?" Gratification caught Jermyn off balance. "She didn't tell me that."

"She wouldn't." He examined the horizon, now almost invisible in the gathering darkness. "She said, in fact, that your familiar showed far better discipline than you did and is thus obviously as much a credit to your training as you are not to mine."

"Oh." It took Jermyn a moment to work that out. When he did, he was indignant on Master Eschar's behalf. "It isn't your fault. You taught me well, Aunt Merry always said—"

"Yes." Eschar stared unsmilingly out into the darkness. "Jean knows perfectly well why I haven't beaten magical discipline into you, my boy. I genuinely lack the ability to impose such discipline. If I were a practicing wizard, it would be different. But then, if I were a practicing wizard, we would probably neither of us be here."

Jermyn was prepared to give him an argument. "She says I don't have any discipline."

Eschar raised his eyebrows. "*Any?*"

"Well, she says I don't have *enough* discipline," Jermyn said. The comment rankled a little. "She talked to me as if I were a child."

"She may have a point," the Theoretician said dryly.

Jermyn flushed. "I'm sorry, Master. I guess I am being childish. A little. It's just—well . . ."

"The student always reflects on the teacher, to some extent," Eschar said meditatively. "Don't worry. You reflect very well on me."

I'm not so sure, Jermyn thought glumly. Aloud, he said, "Master, why doesn't Mistress Allons have a familiar?"

"Because she's old." When Jermyn looked at him blankly, Eschar chided him. "*Think*, Jermyn. Any familiar she might bond to now would inevitably suicide when she died. I'm not surprised she has chosen not to take the risk."

"I didn't think of that," Jermyn said humbly. "But she won't have a cat around either. At all."

"I didn't realize that," Eschar said, knocking the

dottle out of his pipe into the snow. He frowned. "Before we came, it seemed only logical for her not to bother with a familiar anymore, but—Jean was always very fond of her pets. Perhaps she's afraid she'd be tempted to call a familiar to her, if she had an animal about. . . . Yes, that must be it."

"Brianne says her grandmother hasn't worked any real magic since her mother—Brianne's mother—died," Jermyn volunteered, thinking, *And maybe that's part of it. Maybe Mistress Allons is afraid* Brianne *would call a familiar, too.*

"What?" Eschar looked up sharply. "Not at all? She's long retired, naturally, but I'd assumed—are you sure?"

Jermyn shrugged. "Brianne seemed to be. I suppose it depends on what she meant by 'real' magic, though."

"In any case, it's disturbing," Eschar said slowly. "I would have expected Jean to keep up with her experiments, at least. I confess, I was surprised to find her so altered by the years."

"What do you mean?"

Eschar's frown deepened. "It's difficult to put it into words. Jean Allons—the Jean Allons I remember—was a vital, charming woman with a keen wit and a lively sense of the ridiculous. She would have scolded you properly and thoroughly over the incident in the conservatory, but she would have laughed over it with me. *At* me."

"And she didn't," Jermyn said, not asking a question.

"Not at all." The concern in the Theoretician's voice was palpable. "She just seemed—tired."

"I—I guess maybe she was," he said, worried because Master Eschar seemed worried. *Should I tell him about Brianne's lessons? But if Lady Jean knows, she doesn't seem to mind. And if she doesn't know, won't that just make things worse?* Uncertainty made his head hurt. "She is pretty old. Maybe it's just that."

"Perhaps," Eschar said, his expression barely visible in the dim light. "The years slip away from us. Jean stopped coming to the city, and I never seemed to find the time to travel north. We corresponded, of course, but mostly about scholarship—not personal matters. Still, she seemed willing enough to be your journeyman-master when I suggested it; delighted, in fact, that I'd found her a student worth teaching. Now—I don't know."

They stood in silence for a moment, watching Delia play in the snow.

"Jean did take the death of her daughter hard," Eschar said finally. "But I thought she'd recovered. And I'd no idea that the situation with Eben was so unpleasant."

"Will you be staying longer than you'd planned, then?" Jermyn asked half-hopefully. If Master Eschar was worried, maybe he'd stay.

"I'm afraid I can't," the Theoretician said, dashing Jermyn's hopes. "If I don't start back in a day or so, I'll be trapped up here by the winter storms —and I do have *some* responsibilities that cannot be abandoned for so long."

"I'll miss you."

Eschar smiled. "I'll miss you too, lad. I'll even miss Delia making nests out of my papers."

"She only did that once."

"I was joking." Master Eschar tucked his pipe inside his tunic.

"I wish Aunt Merry were here," Jermyn said impulsively.

"So do I," Eschar said, sighing. "I wonder what she'd make of Tower Landing? I'll tell her you miss her—and I will *not* mention the tea party, if I can avoid it. You might want to write a letter for me to take back to her."

"I'll do it tomorrow," Jermyn promised. "Just in case you have to leave early."

It was full dark by the time they went in, a snow-soaked Delia wriggling happily in Jermyn's arms so she wouldn't drip on the carpets. Jermyn tried not to think about how he would feel when Master Eschar left for the city, how alone and cut off and on his own.

The last thing the Theoretician said to him, as they parted in the hallway, was a request and a warning. "Jermyn . . . watch out for her, will you?"

"I—I don't . . ."

"Jean and I are old friends," he went on. "I owe her more than I can ever repay. If something happens—if you think I can help—let me know. Somehow. Please?"

"Yes, sir," Jermyn said, wondering dismally how he was going to keep that promise—and if he were already breaking it by keeping Brianne's secret. "That is, I'll try."

5

LEARNING DISCIPLINE

MASTER ESCHAR left the next evening, with the turning of the tide. Everything was so rushed that Jermyn barely had time to scribble a note to his aunt before saying good-bye.

When the *Dawn Voyager* had disappeared across the horizon, Jermyn's real work began. Over the next month, Mistress Allons kept him busy outlining and charting spells. His hand ached with writer's cramp, and his eyes blurred from long hours of copying. He filled first one of the new workbooks, then two, and finally three with the material. But Mistress Allons didn't let him *try* a single spell. She was quite strict about that. "No sorcery. When you have demonstrated that you have begun to discipline yourself, then we will begin. Not until then."

He did try to speak to Brianne once or twice, but finding her alone proved nearly impossible. He suspected she was avoiding him, and he would have worried even more, except that the winter storms had hit in earnest. No one sane would leave the tower alone and on foot, and he was fairly certain that Brianne wasn't crazy.

Delia, at least, was settling in happily. He took her for daily walks in the gardens, which she enjoyed tremendously. While he was still working off his punishment, she would happily prowl the wood-pile as he chopped wood—he had to be firm about her not wandering off into the forest again—and she spent several hours a day in the conservatory. Phineas even became quite fond of her and brought her little treats from the kitchen.

Lady Jean was not interested in Delia at all.

"Your familiar is *your* responsibility," she said. "My only requirement is that she does not disturb my staff."

"I know, Mistress," he said, opening his work-book. "She hasn't. She won't."

"See to it," she told him, not looking up from the book she was annotating. "Have you finished the descant tables?"

"Uh—almost." He bent his head over the row

of figures that he was currently copying. Again. *I've copied this set so many times, I might almost have them memorized*, he thought gloomily. "Mistress Allons . . ."

"Yes, Jermyn?"

He supposed he ought to be encouraged by the fact that she'd started calling him by his first name, but he wasn't. Her tone made him feel about six years old, and a clumsy and unsatisfactory six, at that. "Why am I spending so much time copying descants?"

"Because there is no better way to make sure you remember them," she said.

He was allowed to ask her questions, but he was not allowed to disagree. Still, she didn't object to discussing matters of fact. "Then should I memorize them? I tried that once, and Aunt Merovice said—"

He halted abruptly. Lady Jean looked up. "What did your aunt say?"

"She told me it wasn't necessary to memorize the descant tables," he said at last. *If she takes that as a criticism—or if she says something nasty about Aunt Merry. . . .*

He wasn't sure which possibility upset him more.

Her expression bland, Lady Jean returned to her book. "Work it out for yourself. Do you *need* to memorize them? What are they for?"

Puzzled, Jermyn frowned at the long list of tables. *What are descants for? Well, they're used to figure magical proportions. When you're casting a spell, you have to know how much force to apply to each part of it and how to balance the whole thing. Too much on one side, or too little on another, and the spell will collapse on you. That's why most spells are sold with descant tables included.* He hesitated, then plunged on. *But as a spellmaker I'll need to figure those things out for myself. Oh . . .*

"I don't need to memorize the actual numbers," he said slowly. "Because they'll be different for every spell. But I need to be able to remember the patterns, so I can figure things out when I make my own spells. Especially when I'm creating a spell at the same time I'm working it—I'll need to be able to see how the parts of it ought to fit together."

"Very good," she said, turning a page. He blushed. It was the first compliment she'd given him. "Tomorrow we will start proportional analysis."

Proportional analysis meant that he got to create his own spells—on paper.

"You have a commission for a shield spell," Lady Jean would say as the day began. "A spell much like the one you used in the conservatory, only more versatile. Since your first version might not be appropriate for the spellcaster with whom you are working, have several for him to choose from. At least three."

Or she would point at a picture of a hex symbol drawn in the margins of one of her books. "That's the spell pattern you want to use. What sort of magic would fit best with the octagonal configuration? Where would you put the four elements, and how would you balance them?"

It was more interesting than copying, but harder. He fell asleep at night with the symbols burning and twisting in his brain, woke up in the morning with headachy memories of fantastic spells. Lady Jean never tested any of the spells that he created, at least not that he could see. Once she pinned a version of the shield spell to a board and left it there for three days, until he finally went to her and asked her to take it down.

"Why?" she asked.

"Because it's wrong," he said. It made him uncomfortable to look at it now. "The lines of binding would get out of control if I tried to cast it outdoors."

She regarded him steadily. "How do you know?"

He squirmed. "I just—*see* it. The earth sign is undervalued, and air is too strong. It's clumsy, it's ugly, and it won't work right."

"True." She nodded. "I'm glad you see it. Take the copy down and destroy it—but I would like to see a new version by tomorrow afternoon."

He hesitated. "I don't know if I can by tomorrow afternoon. There's something wrong, and I can't figure out exactly what."

"Then take as long as you need—don't bring me the spell until you are satisfied with it." She leaned forward and wrote a name on a slip of paper. "Try studying Aristei after you are finished with today's exercises. He may give you the insight that you require."

Puzzled, he took the slip and looked at it. "Where?"

"In the big library, under 'Art History.'"

Aristei turned out to be a famous painter whose works were reproduced in one of Lady Jean's books. Jermyn couldn't figure out what he might have to do with a faulty shield spell, but he dutifully went to the library after dinner and pulled the volume off the shelves to look at it. The shield spell didn't seem to get better, but he kept working on it, coming up with several new versions as the days passed. Some were better than others, but none was as good as the spell could be. He spent most evenings in the library, reading the various works suggested by Lady Jean. The big book-lined room was quiet and comfortable, and somehow more cheerful than his own workroom.

Delia went with him. She liked the library almost as much as she liked the conservatory.

You like the dishes filled with candy and nuts on the sideboard, he scolded her.

Um-hm, she admitted shamelessly, nuzzling the covered glass. *More?*

"No, you can't have any more tonight, you little beggar," he said. "Do you want to get fat? Get away from there."

Jermyn was in the library reading a rare first edition of Kates's *On the Art of Spellmaking,* about six weeks after Master Eschar had left, when the situation with Brianne finally began to change.

He had been feeling slightly more confident for the past few days. For one thing, Lady Jean seemed pleased with his work on proportional analysis; he really thought he was beginning to feel his way to a few answers—maybe even to a final version of the shield spell, eventually. For another thing, Delia had caught three large rats in the conservatory and had been extravagantly praised for it by old Phineas.

Kates, however, was not the most lucid of texts.

More than most magical persuasions, spellmaking is an art, the old Master Wizard had written. *The practice of this art, as of all arts, requires skill, knowledge, and understanding, as well as observation and experiment—the tools of science. These things assist the spellmaker in the practice of his profession as a comprehension of the laws of perspective and studies in anatomy benefit the painter....*

"Now, what does that mean?" Jermyn said in frustration.

Pretty words, Delia observed, from his lap.

"Oh, they *sound* nice—very poetic—but this is a textbook! It isn't supposed to be poetic. It's supposed to make sense."

As he glared at the offending page, the side door to the library opened, and Brianne came in. "Oh! Jermyn, I didn't know you were here. I'll come back—"

"That's all right," he said, glancing up. She was alone—this was his chance. "I don't know what I'm doing here anyway. Did you want a book?"

"No, I—I was just going to check that Flora dusted properly today," she said, looking away guiltily.

Jermyn's eyes narrowed slightly. *Powers! She does look like that sketch of her mother. And like her grandmother, too. I never noticed before, but her cheekbones are exactly the same—and the shape of her eyes, and her mouth.* "At this time of the evening?"

"Well, I just didn't have a moment before," she said, defiantly marching to the bookshelves and beginning to run a finger along them. "Tch, look at what she's missed."

"Oh, give it up, Bri," Jermyn said, sighing. "I can see the book in your skirt pocket. What have you been doing—sneaking books on magic to study?"

She whirled. "If you knew anything, you'd know that Grandmother keeps the books on magic in her workroom. I can't get at the really useful books, like the ones *you* read. I just—this is just—"

"Show me," he said, pushing away from the table. *If she thinks Kates would be useful, maybe I ought to lend it to her. That'd teach her.* Delia pattered along the tabletop after him.

Brianne looked like she wanted to argue, but then she gave in and handed it to him. "Here, if you must know. But be quick—I can't stay in the library too long, or Father will start to wonder what I'm up to in here."

"I know," Jermyn said, absently turning the book in his hands. "*Coville's Practical Guide to Magic*—that's no good. It's just a general description. You'd get more out of a decent encyclopedia."

Her shoulders drooped. "I've read the encyclopedia. Everything about magic I could find. But I can't go to Maudie in the winter, and I have to do *something*."

"You aren't going to the hedgewitch's anymore?" Jermyn said, relieved. "I'm glad."

"I know you've been watching me since before

the tea party, so don't bother trying to be polite," she told him.

"I—ah, well," he cleared his throat. "It really wasn't a very good idea, you know."

"No, I don't know," she corrected him. "And in the spring I'm going back again—so there!"

She turned to leave the room, and Jermyn caught her arm. "Wait! Look, I'm sorry about—about everything. But I haven't given you away."

"No," she said slowly. "You haven't. I've been wondering why not."

He shrugged. "I couldn't figure out what was the best thing to do, so I just kept my mouth shut."

There was a silence, then Brianne broke it. "I suppose I ought to thank you."

"You don't have to," he said, a little annoyed.

"No—I do thank you. I mean it," she insisted, pushing a thick lock of hair off of her forehead. "It's just—I feel so awful! No one pays much attention to me in winter. There's no real entertaining anywhere in the district. Except for Solstice Rites, I could be studying almost all the time—if I knew *what* to study."

"What does the Solstice have to do with anything?" he asked.

"I always help Uncle Eben with the decorations, and with food for the Table for Strangers," she said, taking the little book back from him and putting it on a shelf. "He's all alone, and Solstice is a lot of work for one priest. Even in a little place like Land's End."

"I suppose it is," he said. He'd never thought about it. "You should have told me. I could help."

"When?" Her smile was a little forced. "You've been studying and working so hard, you've scarcely had time to sleep."

"Yes, but—" He hesitated. "Look, if you really want to read about magic, don't waste your time on books like the *Practical Guide*. That's a book for children. I read it in dame school."

"I told you, Gran keeps all the real books on magic in her workroom," she said impatiently.

"She keeps the grimoires and the rare books like Kates in her workroom most of the time," he corrected her. "The rest of the standard theoretical texts are down here. Why don't you try some personal accounts? They could tell you a lot, and they'd be more interesting reading, too."

"Like what?"

"Like—oh, like the Hortensius diaries. Mistress Allons must have a copy of those. Master Eschar says they're basic." He scanned the shelves. "They'd be in 'Personal History,' or maybe 'Biography.'"

Lady Jean had not one but two editions of the diaries. Brianne selected the one-volume set, after blowing the dust off of it. "I really do need to talk to Flora. Thanks, Jermyn. I never would have thought of Personal History."

"No charge," he said, grinning in relief. It certainly wouldn't do Brianne any harm to read Hortensius—not like visiting a hedgewitch.

After that, his relationship with Brianne steadily improved. She came into the library every few evenings, to get his suggestions about what to read next. Eventually she started to find her way around for herself, much as he had when he'd first rummaged in Master Eschar's library as an apprentice, but she still usually came in when he was there. She said that if her father saw her and wondered what she was doing, she could always say she'd come to ask if Jermyn needed anything. Jermyn didn't mind. He was beginning to like Brianne—a lot.

So was Delia. *Nice yellowhair*, she said, picturing Brianne's sandy blond hair looking like a windblown dandelion in late summer.

And besides, she lets you eat all the walnuts and cashews out of the library bowls, he said, amused but pleased. Delia sniffed.

Sometimes he went with Brianne to the village. Lady Jean didn't seem to object. She even started giving Jermyn errands to do for her there. He thought that was what she wanted when she called him to her workroom after breakfast a few days before Solstice.

It wasn't.

"No," she said, when he asked her. "I have no need of anything in the village. If you would open the crystal, please?"

"You want me to practice working your crystal?" he asked, delighted at the prospect. It would be the first time she'd suggested that he actually use his magical abilities since he'd come north.

"Of course I don't want you to practice working the crystal, silly boy," she snapped. "Someone appears to be trying to speak through it to you, which means that you will have to be here to receive the message. Now, unwrap that—that useless piece of rock and let's get this over with."

"Someone's calling me? Who—" He stopped, suddenly aware of who it must be. *Master Eschar can't use a crystal himself, and he'd ask whoever was relaying for him to talk to Lady Jean first anyway. That leaves—oh, no.*

Hoping against hope that he was wrong, Jermyn unfolded the ends of the velvet cloth, leaving the crystal set in the center of it. Light from the window caught the facets and created a forest of flickering rainbows against the glass cases along the opposite wall. His eyes widened: Lady Jean's crystal was almost twice the size of any he'd seen before. It was also very old; the sharp edges of the facets were worn round with age. Gently, he reached out to run his hand across its surface, sensing the dim light within that meant another wizard was trying to reach into the web of crystalline energy.

"Not yet," Lady Jean said sharply. "We'll go in together—in link."

He looked at her, affronted. "I won't hurt it. I've been using my aunt's crystal since I was seven years old."

"We'll go in together," she repeated. Her dark blue eyes were distant, incalculable; and it was *her* crystal. Unwillingly, he nodded.

"I'm not used to working a crystal in link with anyone but my aunt," he warned her. "She says I've got a rough touch."

A wintry smile gleamed briefly in Lady Jean's eyes. "I'll chance it," she said, reaching out with her left hand. He took it in his right hand and tentatively set his own left on the cut surface of the crystal.

Careful, now, he told himself. *Wake it slowly. Whoever is there should be expecting you, and you don't want to give—anyone—a headache.* He sent his mind out, reaching into the delicate silver web of energies emanating from the core of the crystal. Its facets became lines in the air, extending out and crossing and recrossing until the crystal itself was the glowing center of a wilderness of gleaming pathways, a maze of magic.

He'd never seen so many lines. For an instant, he panicked, afraid he'd lose his way in the web. Then he sensed Lady Jean's presence beside him.

Don't push, she said, her mental voice as tart and commanding as her spoken one. *Follow that line to the center—there. See?*

One silver thread brightened, thickened, as he and Lady Jean both fastened their attention on it. Gratefully, Jermyn began to edge down it. As he did, he sensed the first tendrils of a very familiar presence.

It was his aunt, of course. Who else? He'd missed her, had wanted to call her, but he hadn't thought that *she* might call him. *Checking up on me, as if I were a child spending the night away from home for the first time*, he fumed, very privately. *How could she humiliate me like this?*

Into the crystal, he called, *Aunt Merry? Aunt Merovice, is that you?*

For a long moment, he thought that he'd guessed wrong—or that he wouldn't get through. The contact was thinner than any he'd ever known, but finally Merovice Graves took shape in the crystal. A small, round woman, she looked up at him through the crystal with a concerned expression on her face. She was wearing her best flowered print dress with lace, the one she'd bought to celebrate his finishing his apprenticeship. At the sight of her, Jermyn forgot all about being embarrassed. Instead, overcome by a sudden wave of homesickness, he fought to blink back tears.

"I'm here, Aunt," he said around the lump in his throat.

"It *is* you, Jerry!" she said. "I've been calling and calling—why didn't you answer?"

"I did answer," he said. *And of course she begins with a question. She'll never change.* "Just now. Lady Jean and I—"

"Oh? Is she with you?" She peered up through one of the facets of the crystal, for all the world as if she were looking through a tiny window. "Why doesn't she speak for herself, then? I can't tell—yes, someone's there, but it isn't clear. Well, give her my best, if it's her."

"I will," Jermyn said. "What do you want, Aunt? Are you feeling all right? Have you seen Master Eschar?"

She looked insulted; questions about her health always irritated her. "Of course I'm feeling fine. So is Pol, and William had dinner here just the other night. He's nothing but skin and bones, the man frets so, but he's too stubborn for anything to be truly *wrong* with him."

"Then why are you calling?" he asked, interrupting the flow of words.

"Because I wanted to know if *you* were all right!" she said. "I hadn't heard from you in so long—"

"I wrote," he protested. "I sent a letter with Master Eschar."

"Snippy little I'm-fine-and-how-are-you note. I wouldn't call it a *letter*. And then—nothing. With William so dour he'll scarce say a word about you or that northern wilderness, what *was* I to think but that something was amiss?"

"Well, nothing is," he said, more sharply than he'd intended. He had to cut her off—he didn't want her to start asking about Master Eschar's worries, not with Lady Jean sitting right beside him. "I've just been busy."

She sniffed. "Of course you've been busy. Have you been eating right? You look pale."

"I'm fine," he assured her awkwardly. "It's just the crystal. I'm surprised the image will carry so far."

"I'm not," she said. "I did think you might have difficulty making the initial reach—"

"Aunt, you *know* I can use a crystal," he said.

"Yes, well, why else wouldn't you have called me before now?" she asked logically. "Not that it matters. Now that I've made first touch, you should be able to reach me again easily enough."

"Yes, well, maybe." He looked uneasily at Lady Jean, who didn't flicker an eyelid. "Aunt, I promise I'll—I'll stay in touch. I'll write more letters. Longer ones. But maybe—maybe you shouldn't call me like this again."

"What!" For an instant she looked hurt, then her eyes narrowed. "Hmm. Like that, is it? I own, I'd wondered. So William was right. . . ."

Jermyn straightened in alarm. When Merovice got that calculating look in her eyes, there was no telling what she might be considering. "Aunt Merry, please don't—don't think—"

"Now, now, don't worry," she said briskly. "You can trust me. No doubt I interrupted your studies. Tell Her Ladyship that I won't do so again. Sitting by you and listening, is she? Funny, I can scarcely sense her—I imagine she's having some difficulty sensing me, as well, though of course she can hear whatever *you* say. Behave yourself, then, boy, and tell that little beast of yours to behave herself too. You hear me, Jerry?"

"I hear you, Aunt," he said, glancing sidelong at Lady Jean. She didn't seem to have noticed anything. *Maybe Aunt Merry's right—maybe I can hear her, but for some reason Lady Jean can't. Still, I'll bet she asks me why Aunt Merry called. I'd better try to explain first.* "We miss you, too."

She grinned at him, but her forehead was wrinkled, and her eyes were dark with concern. "Can't fool you, can I, Nephew? Well, I won't try. Write me—and use the crystal when you *can*."

The emphasis on her last word lingered in the air as her image in the crystal started to dissolve back into an amorphous spark of brightness. Unthinkingly, Jermyn grimaced at it. He should have written Aunt Merry again, but he hadn't known what to say. *Did Master Eschar know she was going to call me?* he wondered. *Well, if he didn't know, I bet he gets an earful by sunset.* But he suddenly realized, feeling like a fool, that the Theoretician must have intended him to try to keep in touch through Aunt Merry.

"You may disengage the crystal now, Jermyn," Lady Jean's voice said beside him.

"Yes, ma'am," he said. "I'm sorry about my aunt—I'm sure she didn't mean to intrude. She didn't know you weren't letting me do magic."

Try as he might, he couldn't keep the irritation out of his voice.

"Working a crystal is hardly serious magic," Lady Jean said calmly. "Unless you mean to leave the web gathering strength like that all day."

"Yes, ma'am," he said again, chastened.

The depths of the crystal had begun to glow a cloudy white. Jermyn reached into the energy web and slowly began to sever his connections to it, one thread at a time. The disengagement was always the most difficult part of the operation for him: He hated this patient one-strand-at-a-time stuff. It would be so much easier to sweep all the threads up into one bunch and twist them together like a rope, but that would leave a mess for the next time he used the crystal. *If I ever get another chance*, he thought.

Well, at least she sees I do know what I'm doing. Maybe next time I can talk to Aunt Merry privately.

Then the mist in the crystal hardened, began to pulse with new light. It took him by surprise, fastening sharp tendrils into the pathways of his mind, holding him hard. Frightened, he pulled against it and gasped as hot agony shot through him. *What? Why? It hurts! No crystal should hurt—*

His head pounded in rhythm to the light in his mind. Desperately he reached out for Delia, to draw strength through her to fight this entrapment, but he couldn't reach her. He could find the thread of the familiar bond, but he couldn't concentrate enough to follow it home. *Where is she? I can't work magic without her. Let go of me! Let go!*

Jermyn! Lady Jean's voice came from impossibly far away. *Don't try to pull. Cut it! Cut the thread!*

It was like being held by silvery spiderwebs that grew stronger every second. The glow at the center of the crystal gathered strength, pulling all the strands of the web into it; at its core, Jermyn dimly sensed, was a spreading stain of red against silver, as rich as soft velvet and as wet and warm as blood. Frantically, Jermyn fought against it, trying to focus. *Cut the thread? Which thread?* All he could see was haze.

One of the strands of spiderweb flashed with a brief blue glow, the color of Lady Jean's eyes. *That one!* the thought that wasn't his own shouted in his mind. Lashing out wildly, he struggled to visualize the thread snapping. *Use all your strength, whatever is in you—break it!* His hands scrabbled uselessly against the edge of the table as he struggled to obey.

The light flared, its heat flickering over him like rainwater. He watched, frozen, as the still-shimmering crystal rolled off the table to land on the carpet. The thick padding should have cushioned and broken the fall, but somehow it didn't. The brittle sound of glass breaking seemed to shiver through the entire tower as a great jagged piece chipped off one faceted side of the crystal and went spinning out into the center of the room.

6

BROKEN CRYSTAL

JERMYN STARED, appalled, at the ruin of the crystal. He looked at Lady Jean, but she had leaned back in her chair and closed her eyes. Her face was as pale and deeply lined as crumpled paper. *I didn't mean to do that*, he thought numbly. *I didn't know you could get trapped in a crystal, and for one to crack like that—*

"Mistress—" The word came out on a high squeak. He swallowed and tried again. "Mistress Allons, what happened?"

She spoke without opening her eyes, with long pauses between each phrase, as if too many words tired her. "Too much stress . . . cracked the interior framework. I have seen it happen before. Not often."

"What did I *do?*" he asked, trying to calm the queasy feeling in his stomach. *Too much stress? But I didn't feed that much power into the thing. Why, I couldn't even reach Delia before it broke.* "I—I've never—nothing like that has ever happened to me before. Even when I was seven years old, the worst thing I ever did was pull out too suddenly and give myself a splitting headache."

"It's much the same effect," she said, opening her eyes at last. As if moving underwater, she tilted her head to look at him. "You were caught . . . by the spell that powers the crystal. Have you ever looked at crystal spells?"

He shook his head. "No."

"Pity," she said, closing her eyes again. "If you had . . . you might have seen . . ."

"Seen what?" he asked, confused. "Mistress?"

"Jermyn . . ." she said, her voice a dying fall. Frightened at last by her pallor, he bent over her chair and strained to hear the words. "I think . . . the healer . . ."

"Mistress!" he cried, reaching out to touch her shoulder. She slumped sideways in the chair, unconscious.

Jermyn ran.

He met Brianne rushing up the stairs, her eyes wild and her face as pale as her grandmother's. She was wearing the old brown dress she normally put on to oversee housework, and she still had a feather duster in one hand. Delia was right behind her, chittering in anger that Jermyn should work magic without calling on her.

"Gran," she gasped. "I was cleaning the silver and I felt *something* sort of—snap. Is she—"

"I don't know what went wrong," Jermyn said. "Go get the healer, whoever it is. Your grandmother needs—"

"The healer is Jemima Kestrell," Brianne said, turning back down the stairs without missing a beat. "She'd be in the village this morning—I'll send Phineas. You stay with Gran."

Bad Je'm'n! Delia said, sitting on her hindquarters to claw at his leg. *Bad magic! All ugly.*

"I know, Dee," he whispered, bending to pick her up. Her warm weight was comforting. "I'm sorry—I should have warned you, but there wasn't time."

Delia hissed, her back arching with annoyance. *Bad, bad!* Then she nuzzled his chin forgivingly. *Scared? Whyfor?*

"Because. I don't know." He squared his shoulders and walked back into the workroom: Mistress Allons was still slumped motionless in her chair.

Delia let out a squeak of surprise. *Lady!*

"Yes. She fainted, I think." He set Delia on the floor, where she padded over to sniff at the fragment of broken crystal. Once she was sure he was all right, she became intensely curious.

"Careful," he warned, most of his attention on his journeyman-master. "It's sharp."

She's breathing all right, I think, he thought, hovering anxiously over Lady Jean. *At least, I can see the lace move. If only I had some smelling salts. Should I try to loosen her clothes? I wish I could get her over to the sofa.*

He compromised by unbuttoning her lace collar, feeling that to do any more would be to take liberties. Her skin felt cold and clammy to the touch.

"What is going on in this house?" Duncan Campbell shouted from behind him.

Jermyn jumped, and he only just warned Delia before she went into her defensive posture.

"The lights in my study have been flickering for this half hour. How can you expect me to get any work done with this kind of—*Mother!*"

Jermyn straightened wearily to face him.

"She fainted when I broke the crystal," he said simply. "Brianne is sending for the healer. I don't know *how* it happened exactly, but there was a lot of energy in the spell when I released it. The overflow must be disrupting the household spells. They should settle down in a minute or two."

"You—broke—the—crystal?" Duncan swelled, seeming almost to double in size—like a small green frog Jermyn had seen once. "That crystal was an heirloom. It's been in the family for decades. It—it shouldn't—Mother?"

Lady Jean stirred. "Eben?" she said, her voice very weak. "Eben, where are you?"

Duncan rushed to kneel by her chair and chafe her wrists. "It's Duncan, Mother. Do you want Eben? Shall I send for him?"

"No. . . ."

"Mother? Are you all right?" her son-in-law asked.

"Maybe she should be in bed," Jermyn suggested, trying not to hover himself.

"The healer—"

"I've sent for Jemima, Father," Brianne said from the doorway. She was still pale, but very composed. "She'll be here soon. In the meanwhile, Jermyn's right—we should get Gran to bed. I've brought Tim and Arrick from the stable. They'll help."

The two burly workmen behind her nodded in hesitant agreement.

"Yes, of course, of course," Duncan said. He stopped fussing and supervised the removal of Lady

Jean to her bedchamber, where Brianne thanked them and then firmly shut the door in all of their faces.

The two workmen vanished, leaving Jermyn alone with Brianne's father.

"I hope you're satisfied," Duncan said in a hard voice. "This is all your fault."

Jermyn felt as if he'd been punched in the stomach. Crouched between his feet, Delia hissed.

"I know," he said, his mouth dry. "But I don't know what I did wrong."

"Not whatever you did today," Duncan said impatiently. "It's your training in general. My mother-in-law is not a well woman. Your training could be the death of her."

"What do you mean?"

"What I said," Duncan told him. "Or is plain speaking beyond you Guild wizards? She has been warned that even the practice of simple magic is now beyond her strength. The healers say that if she refrains from sorcery, she can live for years yet. If she does not—well. . . ."

"I don't believe it," Jermyn said, stunned. "If that's true, why did she accept me as her journeyman? She must have known she'd have to work magic to train me."

"She considers it her duty, naturally," Duncan said stiffly. "She has always done her duty by the Wizards' Guild. However, if you ask me—"

Jermyn took a deep breath, and let it out slowly. He wanted to say something to throw Duncan's own words back at him, but he couldn't think of anything. *It* can't *be true*, he thought. *Master Eschar would know—the Guild would never permit her to take such a risk. But she was so pale. . . .*

"Come on, Dee," he said. Leaving Duncan standing in the hall, he turned on his heel and headed back to the workroom. He knew he was being rude, but he didn't care. Delia followed, pausing only long enough for one last hiss at Duncan.

The workroom door had been left open; Jermyn stood in the doorway for a moment, surveying the room without really seeing it. He didn't know what he wanted to find—proof that Duncan was wrong? If that was it, he was looking in the wrong place; there was nothing waiting for him in the workroom but the pieces of shattered crystal.

Automatically he bent to pick up the broken fragment from the carpet. The crystal edge caught his palm, slicing into the flesh.

"Ouch!" Dismayed, he stared at the blood welling from the scratch.

Je'm'n! Sharp. Curled primly at the edge of the rug, Delia gave him back his own warning.

"I know it's sharp, silly," he said, annoyed. "I just didn't know it was *that* sharp. It's like a razor."

He hunted around the room until he found a pair of yellow leather gloves rolled into a ball on one of the open shelves. The gloves were stained and creased, cut in more than one place; obviously, they were working gloves. They were tight, but the worn leather stretched to fit his hands. Wearing the gloves, he carefully picked up the broken piece of crystal and carried it over to the larger section on the table. When he tried to fit the two together, the crystal grated against itself, chiming off-key. Hastily, he pulled the segments apart and set them side by side.

The pieces sat on the velvet cloth, soaking up all the light in the room and making broken rainbows of reflected sun on the walls. A drop of blood darkened the edge of the broken piece, smearing it unpleasantly. Jermyn pulled the gloves off and set them down on the table, wincing a little as he pulled at the still-bleeding cut. His hand throbbed.

Ignoring the pain, he focused on the crystal. *I wonder if it can be mended? If it can't, we're cut off from the city and the Guild, for sure, unless someone else has a crystal. Eben? He's a priest, but he trained as a wizard once. Or maybe the healer. . . .*

Delia left her sniffing around the rug and butted his leg. He bent down and hauled her into his arms. *Bad*, she said, her mind voice troubled. *Bad magic.*

"Yes, it was," he said.

There was a noise in the hall. He looked up

quickly as Brianne and a woman carrying a healer's bag came into the room. Brianne looked sober but composed.

"He should be in the workroom, Jemima," she was saying over her shoulder as they came through the door. "At least, I don't think he would have left the door open and the room empty. Jermyn?"

"I'm here," he said, swinging around to face her. "Is Mistress Allons all right?"

"Jemima says she'll be fine," Brianne said. "She's sleeping. This is the healer, Jemima Kestrell. You met her parents at the tea party, I think. She wants to ask you a few questions—why, you've cut yourself."

"It's nothing," he said, stuffing the injured hand into his pocket. "I was just picking up the broken crystal. It doesn't hurt."

"It does," the healer corrected him, moving forward. "Though you're probably right that it is nothing serious. May I look at it?"

"Uh, sure." He couldn't think of any reason why not.

"Sit in the chair by the window, then, so I can see what I'm doing."

Jemima Kestrell was a tall woman, lean and competent looking. She had a long thin face with fine features and arched brows. Her dark hair was tied back in a knot, and her soft gray skirts and tunic—while workmanlike and presentable—seemed just slightly disorganized. But she smiled at him, her brown eyes understanding, her healer's touch warm and soothing. Jermyn leaned back in his chair, feeling himself begin to relax. Delia put her forepaws on the arm of the chair to watch suspiciously, and the healer smiled at her, too.

"No, not bad at all," Jemima said presently. She held his hand between both of hers gently, and he felt the pain begin to disappear. "There, that should get it started. The bleeding has almost stopped. Best to let your body go the rest of the way itself. Do you mind a bandage for a day or so?"

"No," he said, shaking his head.

"Good." She reached into her bag. "I'll use a liniment, too, but the bandage will help keep the cut clean. It will also remind you to be careful. Sorry, this may sting a bit."

It did, but not nearly as much as the cut itself had hurt. Jermyn bit his lip briefly and the pain was gone.

"Thank you," he said, holding up his bandaged hand to look at it. Then he glanced from the healer to Brianne, who was sitting in her grandmother's chair on the other side of the table. "You did say Mistress Allons was all right?"

"She is," Jemima said, nodding reassuringly as she closed her bag. "Just exhausted. What happened?"

"Father says you dropped the crystal and broke

it," Brianne said, pointing at the pieces. "How did you do that?"

"I *didn't* drop it," he told her. "It just—sort of rolled off the table and cracked, all by itself. I got caught in the web, and I couldn't get out. Mistress Allons guided me—we were linked—and then the crystal broke."

Brianne frowned. "What web?"

"The web of energy connecting this crystal to other crystals," Jemima told her. "A wizard activates his section of the web and then reaches out through it to touch the web of another wizard's crystal—that's how these things work."

"Oh." She subsided, looking thoughtful. "I didn't know that."

"I'm not too clear on the process myself," Jemima remarked. "I can use crystals, but I don't really understand them. The activation spell is the affair of the Wizards' Guild, not the Healers'. For what it's worth, I've never heard of a crystal breaking from within."

"Mistress Allons said there was too much stress on the interior framework," Jermyn offered. "Right before she fainted."

"Whatever that means." Jemima shook her head, her thin features looking concerned.

"I think it's got something to do with the spell that powers the crystal," he said. "With the amount of power actually *in* the spell."

"That still doesn't mean much to me," she said. "I'll have to ask Eben. Maybe he'll be able to explain."

"Journeywoman Kestrell—"

"Oh, call me Jemima, lad," the healer said. "Journeyman to journeyman."

Jermyn almost managed a smile. "I guess I'm not used to being a journeyman myself yet."

"It takes a while. What did you want to ask me?"

He glanced quickly at Brianne, who was brooding over the crystal. "Well, it's just that Duncan—Mr. Campbell—says that Mistress Allons has been advised by her healer not to work magic anymore. If you're her healer . . . is it true?"

"I'm Lady Jean's healer and the only healer in Land's End these days," Jemima said, sighing. "And yes, it's more or less true. Jean hasn't worked any powerful magic since—not in years."

"But—but—," Jermyn stuttered. "Why am I here, then? She's going to have to work magic to teach me."

Brianne came to life. "You try telling Gran what she should and shouldn't do."

"Besides, it isn't that clear cut," Jemima said. "Jean is capable of performing minor magics, and of teaching, so long as she doesn't overdo things and rests frequently. When Master Eschar first approached her about your training, she consulted me, and I consulted her former healer in the city. He and I agree—if she's careful, there is little risk."

"You should have heard the fights she had with Father when he found out what she was considering," Brianne put in. "He had a fit. He even tried to get Uncle Eben to do something. In fact, Father actually thought he'd convinced Gran to tell you not to come, which is why he was so surprised when you got here."

"If he's afraid she might kill herself, he has every right to be upset," Jermyn said.

"Oh, don't be silly, Jermyn," Brianne started to say, exasperation in her voice.

Jemima began talking at the same time. "It isn't that bad," she said.

"Are you sure?" he asked worriedly. "If she hasn't worked magic in such a long time, maybe she shouldn't even try."

"She stopped working magic long before her heart started to give out," Jemima said, and closed her lips firmly together as if she'd said too much.

"I already told him about Mother," Brianne said. She looked cool and very calm, but there was a pulse beating in her throat. "And about how Grandmother stopped practicing magic when Mother had her—accident."

"When your mother killed herself, you mean," Duncan said from the doorway, harsh and strained. "Killed herself with magic."

Brianne froze, slumping down into the chair as if she were trying to hide herself in its cushions. Jemima leaned back against the table and looked at the ceiling. "Hello, Duncan," she said. "How are you today? It's nice to see you."

Duncan ignored her. "Brianne, you aren't allowed in this room. Go to your bedchamber—at once!"

"Hello, Jemima. I'm very well, thank you," the healer went on. "And how did you find my mother-in-law this fine day?"

Brianne swallowed. "Father, I—"

"I ordered you to leave!" he thundered.

"How can she, when you're standing in the only doorway?" Jermyn pointed out—reasonably, he thought. Duncan flushed with anger.

Jemima chuckled. "Very true," she said. She looked at Duncan, shook her head, and sighed. "Well, we've tried common courtesy and not gotten anywhere. Maybe rudeness will do the trick. Duncan, your disciplinarian act is not necessary. Brianne knows how her mother died as well as you do. Haven't you been telling her about it as a bedtime story for the past twelve years? Behave yourself."

"Stay out of this, Jemima," he said, his voice tight with rage. "This is between my daughter and me."

"I will not stay out of it while you attack your wife's memory," she said, her mouth drawn thin.

"Annalise was my friend, and she did *not* commit suicide."

"I didn't mean—"

"You said that she 'killed herself with magic,' didn't you?" she retorted. "Well, then. Annalise was working with powerful sorcery, and she died—by *accident*. It was terrible, but it could have happened to anyone. I know that, Brianne knows that, and if you had the brains of a butterfly, you would admit you know it, too, and get on with the rest of your life."

"That it could have happened to anyone *is* the problem," Duncan said stiffly. "Brianne, come with me."

"Yes, Father," she said, her voice colorless. She stood up. "Jermyn, will you see the room is sealed? Jemima, I'm sorry I can't show you out."

"That's all right, child, I know the way," she said, her voice rueful. "I'll see you again. Sometime."

When Brianne and Duncan had left, there was a little silence. Jermyn broke it.

"How do I seal the room?" he asked, annoyed. "I haven't got a key."

Jemima looked surprised. "Just pull the door closed behind you and make certain that the lock catches. Her ladyship's own protections will take over then."

114

"Oh." Jermyn felt foolish. "I should have known that."

"Yes, you should—journeyman," she said, looking around. "Well, I have everything. Is there anything you need before we leave? You won't be able to get back in on your own if you forget something."

"No, I don't have anything of mine in here," he said. "Except my familiar."

"Speaking of which, I find I'm being rude myself, ignoring one member of our group." She held out one hand for the skunk to sniff delicately. "Hello, Delia. It's nice to meet you."

"How did you know her name?" Jermyn asked, surprised.

"Oh, she's quite famous in the village," Jemima said cheerfully. "I've been hoping you'll bring her visiting, just so I can watch people's reactions."

Jermyn thought about that, then decided he didn't really *want* to think about it. "One of these days. Jemima. . . ."

She stopped, halfway to the door. "Yes?"

"You said you knew Brianne's mother," he blurted out.

"Yes. I knew her." She sighed. "I was younger than she was, but it never seemed to make a difference. In fact, I introduced her to Duncan."

"You did?"

Jemima smiled, remembering. "He was a friend

115

of my brother's, and he came to visit. I asked him to take me to the tower one day, and he and Annalise—well, the rest is history, as they say. It caused quite a stir at the time. She was already a Guild journeyman, and he was just a boy at school, but they never looked back from that first meeting. I don't think Duncan has even begun to recover from her death. He loved her very much."

"What was her Guild speciality?" Jermyn asked, standing up with Delia in his arms. She wriggled to be put down, and he set her at his feet.

"That was part of the problem," Jemima said crisply. "She never settled on one. I think she'd wanted to be a spellmaker, and when that didn't work out, she just—dabbled. That's why she never made it past journeyman, Eben says. She certainly had the strength. But after all, she didn't *need* to work magic for a living."

"I see," Jermyn said thoughtfully. "Was she—what was she like? As a person?"

"You've seen the portrait." Jemima nodded toward the easel. "I wish Her Ladyship would put that away, but I've given up arguing about it. Annalise was like her mother in some ways. Brilliant, forceful, and very, very stubborn. Brianne is her image."

"Does—does Brianne's resemblance to her mother bother Mistress Allons?" Jermyn asked, thinking he might have found the reason why Lady

Jean refused to help her granddaughter study magic.

Jemima hesitated. "Perhaps. At first. Now . . . I don't know. I don't think so. Her Ladyship has always kept her own counsel, and Brianne doesn't confide in me."

"Why not?" They were at the door; Jermyn stood with his hand on the latch, waiting. "Most people trust healers."

She rubbed the back of her neck tiredly. "Duncan's doing, I suspect. He was very possessive when she was a small child; though—to do him justice—he's never tried to interfere between Brianne and her grandmother. Oh, the man's a fool! I wish Eben would do something."

"What could Brianne's uncle do?"

"Something," she said, exasperated. "Anything. He's a son of the house, after all, and he knows as much about magic as anyone who hasn't wound up in the Wizards' Guild. More importantly, Duncan seems to respect him. But Eben won't even try to ease the situation. He says he can't intrude."

Jermyn pulled the door closed and tried it; the lock caught. When he reached out with his other senses, he could feel that the workroom's magical protections had clicked neatly into place as well. "I suppose he means that Lady Jean wouldn't like it."

"Yes, well, she can hardly like the situation as it stands," Jemima said. She shook her head as if to clear it. "I'm sorry, Jermyn. None of this is your problem. Look, I'll be visiting on and off over the next few days, to check on Her Ladyship. I'll see to your hand at the same time."

"Or I could go to see you in the village," he suggested slowly. He liked Jemima. At his feet, Delia agreed. He smiled down at her absently. *Maybe Jemima can help. But I need to talk to Brianne about her before I say anything.*

Jemima cocked her head, looking him up and down. "Hmm. If you wish. Most mornings I'm in the house at the end of the street with the two blue spruces. I make my rounds in the afternoons. If your hand—or anything else—is giving you trouble, drop by and I'll see what I can do."

7

REHEARSAL

JERMYN DID NOT see his journeyman-master again until three days later. He spent the time taking Delia for long walks in the snow-filled gardens, reading, worrying, and wondering. When Lady Jean at last sent for him, he left Delia hunting rats in the conservatory under Phineas's watchful eye and went upstairs immediately. To his surprise, the door to the workroom was half-open. Hesitantly, he knocked.

"Come in," she said, her voice sounding as strong as it had the day she had scolded him after the tea party.

When he entered, she was seated in the same chair, which had been placed by the fire. The table—with the broken crystal still on it—had been pulled over beside her. She was wearing the lace shawl around her shoulders, but that was her only concession to weakness.

"You sent for me, Mistress?" he said.

She looked up as he entered, and he felt a slight shock: She was as taut as a fiddle string.

He wasn't guessing, he *knew*. They had been linked since the day the crystal had broken.

He'd realized what was happening by the morning after the accident—realized that the psychic link between journeyman wizard and master had been established. When a journeyman started to work magic with his master, Jermyn knew, the two talents became as connected as if they shared a joint power. That link allowed a master wizard to train a journeyman directly, through a mental awareness of the journeyman's actions. If Jermyn made a mistake in the course of working magic now, Lady Jean would be able to locate and correct it. If she needed strength for some spell, he would be able to supply it—and would be unable to prevent her from taking it through him, if she wished. She was in control of the bond until Jermyn severed the link, which wouldn't happen until he became a master in his own right.

I knew we'd link eventually, Jermyn thought,

struggling for composure. The connection was stronger now that they were in the same room. *I just didn't think it would happen so soon. And I didn't think it would feel like this, like we're—tied. I thought it would be mostly from her to me, like with Delia.*

He could almost see the blue cord of power pulsing as it stretched between them. Except for color, it looked like the golden familiar-link connecting him to Delia—but frailer, more tenuous.

"I sent for you." Lady Jean's mouth tightened as she looked him up and down. He could feel the stress on the bond between them and wondered if she felt it as sharply as he did. *She should*, he thought, but she didn't refer to it by so much as the flicker of an eyelash. "I'll need you to fetch books for me, from that cabinet."

She pointed at a tall ebonywood cabinet recessed in an inner wall. Tentatively, he tried the handle.

"It's locked," he said.

"Well, of course it's locked," she said. "Do you think I leave all my books lying around where every intrusive visitor might poke at them? You'll find the key in the desk, in a wooden box in the center drawer. It's spelled—bring it to me, please."

The small wooden box was inlaid with ivory. Even inside the desk drawer, it had acquired a layer of dust. He brushed it off and lifted the lid to take out an ornate iron key. When he picked it up, he could feel the spell set into the metal—one he'd never encountered before. *It's old*, he recognized, slightly surprised. *The spell's almost as dusty as the box. It must be a long time since she's gone into that cabinet.*

Lady Jean took the key in her hands, holding it lengthwise, across the palms. Her lips moved slightly as she rehearsed the spell in her mind. Jermyn tried to follow the magic, but he couldn't, even through their link. It went too fast for him, finishing before he had a chance to decipher it.

With a sigh, she leaned back and handed him the key.

"There, that should do it," she said. "You may open the cabinet now."

"That's a very neat spell," he said, sensing the change in the key. *If I weren't already looking for it, I couldn't tell anything was different*, he thought, marveling. *It's so simple, it's complicated.* "Is it one of yours?"

"Yes," she said. "You'll find it in one of the standard texts, though not quite in this form. I believe the Guild refers to it as a privacy spell."

"It's similar to the one you have sealing off the workroom, isn't it?"

She regarded him consideringly. "More or less, though that one is more powerful. I'll need the books on the top shelf—the black volume, to start, and then the others. Bring them to me one at a time, please."

The books she wanted were all old. Some of them had been rebound over the years, but most were large, heavy volumes with cracked spines. One was so heavy that he would have needed to use both hands to carry it even if she hadn't warned him to be careful. Lady Jean paged through the books swiftly, apparently familiar with what was in each. Now and again she made a note in a small workbook she kept in her lap.

After a while, Jermyn ventured a question. "Are you trying to find out something about what happened the other day?"

"Yes," she said shortly. The connection between them fluttered.

Of course she is, he scolded himself. *What else would she be doing?* "Are you looking for crystal spells?"

"No," she said, turning away from him.

"Why don't *I* look for crystal spells, then?" Jermyn asked daringly.

"If you wish," she said, pointing at a bookcase by the window. "Try *Venturi's Encyclopedia,* the section on communication magics."

Venturi's Encyclopedia listed several variants of crystal spells. *I want old versions,* he reasoned, scanning down the pages for references. *It's an old crystal, so the spell should be old, too.*

Apparently the crystal spell had not changed for centuries. About the only differences he could see were that the older spells seemed to be much wider and looser in range, with a greater and more dangerous tendency to soak up any available magical energy.

"Could a crystal spell—an old crystal spell—draw in power from independent sources?" he asked presently.

"Yes."

"That would cause an overload—wouldn't it?"

"Very probably. It depends on the power in question."

Knowing *what* might have happened didn't seem to help with the *how* and *why*. The crystal obviously couldn't have drawn from the spells surrounding Tower Landing, or it would have done so years ago.

Unless it was something I did, Jermyn thought glumly.

At midmorning, Brianne came in with a maid carrying a tray. "Good morning, Grandmother, Jermyn," she said sedately. "Gran, that's enough for today. I've brought you a snack—some fruit and cheese—and then I want you to lie down and rest until lunchtime."

Lady Jean's mouth tightened. "Brianne, I am perfectly all right—"

"I know," her granddaughter interrupted her. "You told Father, and he told Uncle Eben, and then they both had fits. Even after Jemima told them to mind their own business and leave the healing to her. But you do need to rest, and I need Jermyn's help carrying flowers to the village for the Solstice. Please?"

For a moment, he thought Lady Jean was going to refuse, but then the Spellmaker leaned back in her chair.

"I suppose a brief recess is in order." She sounded as if she were humoring a child, but Jermyn could sense the affection as her eyes met Brianne's.

And to think I wondered if she cared for Brianne at all, he thought. *She just doesn't say she does. That makes everything even more confusing.*

"Jermyn, you have my permission to leave the Tower," she went on.

"I really do need help, Jermyn," Brianne urged. "This afternoon is the rehearsal for Solstice Rites, and half of the countryside will be at the church to make certain that Uncle Eben is doing things properly. I promised to bring him some plants from the conservatory for the platform. They have to be wrapped against the cold and carried carefully."

"I'd be glad to come," he said, shutting the book on crystal spells with a snap and setting it on the table for later.

Delia didn't go, mostly because Brianne thought it was a bad idea.

"Not today, Dee," she said, bending to stroke the indignant skunk. "The village will be filled with people from outlying areas. Maybe after Solstice."

Delia sniffed. *Huh. Bad Je'm'n. Not-nice yellowhair.*

"Remember what happened at the tea party?" Jermyn said warningly, sending her an image of Lady Poncebry in hysterics. "We don't want that again. Besides, Phineas says he'll take you hunting while we're gone."

That appeased her. She even consented to staying indoors rather than seeing them off outside. Jermyn thought that that was just as well, since she probably would have spooked the pony. He settled himself in the sleigh and reached to steady the bundles of plants with his free arm.

"Do you think your grandmother will really rest?" he asked.

Brianne shrugged. "Until after lunch. She promised. After that, I doubt it. At least I got her to rest a bit, though, which is more than Father could do."

"Sun's pretty bright," he remarked, looking up at the crisp blue sky.

"Yes, I hope we have such good weather for

Solstice," she said. "It's always depressing when its gloomy and overcast at a festival. Don't look directly at the snow like that. Haven't you ever heard of snow blindness?"

Meekly he shaded his eyes with one hand. "I forgot. You know, Bri, I've been thinking . . . about magic. And you. No, I haven't decided to tell anyone about you," he said, answering the flicker of alarm in her eyes. "I've just been thinking that maybe you should talk to Jemima. She likes you, I can tell. Maybe she could—"

"No," Brianne said, her eyes focusing again on the path. "Not Jemima. Father wouldn't listen to her."

"Why not?" he asked.

"Because Jemima works with magic," she said flatly.

"She's a healer, not a wizard," he protested.

"A healer is close enough for Father," she said. "Jemima uses spells, doesn't she? It would only make things worse if I went to her. Believe me, I know."

There was no arguing with the tone in her voice. *Well, at least now I know exactly why Brianne doesn't confide in Jemima,* he thought as the pony navigated the last gentle slope into Land's End. *For all the good it does me. I guess I'm just going to have to tell Mistress Allons everything—as soon as she's a little stronger.* He wasn't looking forward to it, but somehow the prospect no longer seemed quite so daunting as it used to.

The village was white with new snow. Drifts rimmed the central square, and the little houses and shops were dressed in white up to just beneath their eaves. Brianne drove the pony and sleigh to the smith and started picking up the wrapped plants. Jermyn reached for the largest bundle.

"We don't have to walk far," Brianne said. "Just across the square."

The village church was built of the same dark stone as Tower Landing. It was a small building, no more than two stories high, but it loomed over the rest of Land's End as surely as the tower loomed over the entire landscape. One side boasted a soaring, narrow steeple covered with snow.

The stone steps to the door were cleared of snow, and Jermyn was grateful for the dry footing. Brianne struggled with the heavy door one-handed. Jermyn was about to put down his bundle and help her when the door was pushed open from inside.

Jemima smiled at them from the doorway. "Well, look who's here!" she said. "Brianne, I was going to stop by this afternoon to check on your grandmother."

"I know," Brianne said breathlessly. "I've—that is, *we've* just brought the flowers I promised Uncle Eben."

"Come on in, then, before you and the flowers freeze."

"I brought as many blossoms as Phineas could spare," Brianne told her, leading the way into the interior. "They'll need to be kept cool, but not too cold."

"I've a place all set up in the buttery," Jemima said.

After the brightness outside, the inside of the church seemed as dark as night. Jermyn had a vague impression of wooden benches and faded mosaics as he struggled to avoid tripping on the uneven stone floor. The altar was at the front, its soft alabaster and malachite pillars lifting gracefully out of the gloom. In front of it, in the open place where the Priest would stand to speak, a wooden scaffold was rising: the stage for the Solstice pageant. Eben Allons waved vigorously from around one side. Jermyn tried to free a hand to wave back and couldn't, so he nodded instead. Then he caught sight of Duncan Campbell next to the altar, talking to a short, balding man.

"I didn't know Father was coming to the village today," Brianne remarked.

Jemima glanced up. "Yes, he came back with Eben. He said something about talking to Sig Cammy about repairs at Tower Landing." When Jermyn looked puzzled, she explained: "Sig is the village carpenter. He builds the platform for festivals, and does most of the woodworking in Land's End."

She didn't seem to think it was unusual that Duncan should come to the village without mentioning his intentions to his daughter. Jermyn did, though he couldn't quite figure out why.

The kitchen was bustling with noise and movement and filled with cooking smells. A few of the women looked up and called a greeting as the three of them filed in, but everyone was evidently too busy to do more.

"Over here," Jemima said. "Will this do?"

The buttery was next to the kitchen's outer wall. A woolen tent shielded one corner of it.

"Oh, that's fine, Jemima. That's perfect. We shouldn't lose a single plant if you keep them all in there until tomorrow." She and Jermyn set their bundles down and loosened the wrappings.

"Thank goodness that's taken care of," Jemima said, collapsing into a chair at the kitchen table and motioning to the others to sit. "Would you like a cup of tea?"

"I would, and maybe a biscuit," Brianne said, stripping off her cloak. "Jermyn?"

"No, thank you," he said politely. "Not today."

Brianne laughed. "It's just regular tea, Jermyn. Honest."

Jemima smiled at him. "So you've tried the local

brew, have you? Well, I don't blame you for not wanting more. It's an acquired taste."

They were seated at a table in the breakfast nook, drinking tea and eating fresh butter cookies, when the man Jemima had called the village carpenter came to the door and called. "Ma'am? Missy Jemima? There y'be. D'ye know about those flowers yet?"

Jemima looked up. "What, Sig? Oh, yes, the flowers just came."

"Got to start marking places for 'em," he reminded her. "Scaffold's almost up."

"I'll do it," Brianne said, hastily gulping her tea. "No, Jermyn, you stay here. I'll be right back."

"I'd better come with you," Jemima said, following her out of the kitchen. "Eben told me to show you what he wants . . ."

Jermyn watched them leave. It was good to sit quietly for a moment, not thinking of much of anything. He reached for another cookie.

"More tea, Young Master?" an old voice croaked in his ear. Maudie stood next to the table, a heavy iron kettle in her hands. She had an apron wrapped around the same heavy black dress she'd been wearing the last time he'd seen her. Apparently, she'd been working at the stove, preparing food to put on the Table for Strangers. Her presence startled him somehow, though he wasn't sure why. After all, Maudie lived in Land's End—sort of. She had as much right as anyone to help with Solstice preparations.

"Ah, no, thank you, uh, Mistress," he said, trying to be polite. None of the other women were paying any attention to him, or to Maudie. "I didn't—didn't see you there before. Isn't it a long walk to the village for you?"

She grinned at him sardonically, setting the kettle down on an iron trivet. The rank odor of her in the overheated kitchen almost made him choke. "Long, an' not long. Like the trouble up-long the Tower way just now . . ."

"What do you know about that?" he said suspiciously.

Maudie snorted. "Magic's magic, boy, and power's power. 'Specially with them what touch the land. Can't you see it? Take a look."

Reluctantly, he studied her with his mind's eye. There was something in her, all right, as he'd sensed in the woods—Delia's "smelly magic," hazy but real.

"I see it," he said shortly. "I saw it before. So what?"

She cackled then, a thin, high sound that grated on his nerves. "Yah, so he sees true, does he! Don't close your eyes, Young Master, now they's open. Look and see—whatever's to be seen, by them what follows the land."

She gave him one last sideways glance and moved

away. *What was that all about? If she didn't want anything, why did she talk to me at all?* It had almost sounded as if she were warning him of something. . . .

Suddenly, he realized that he could sense a kind of gathering power in the air. He closed his eyes to try to sort out what his magical senses were telling him. Yes, it was definitely something. It reminded him of—the tea party? Only stronger, more organized. *So I wasn't imagining things then,* he thought, almost pleased to realize it. *But what is Maudie up to now? Mistress Allons said she was harmless. . . . No, she said Maudie wasn't malicious. That isn't exactly the same thing.*

It could be some sort of ritual magic, he supposed—local superstition mixing with festival preparations. He'd read about such things in country provinces. If that was all it was, then it probably *was* harmless. But he didn't think he was going to be able to follow the spell back to its source this time either. The trace was still too faint, too tangled. . . .

A hand landed heavily on his shoulder, and he almost jumped out of his skin.

"Jermyn!" Eben Allons said, smiling broadly. "I'm glad you came with Brianne. Is there any tea left in the kettle?"

"Yes, sir, it's fresh," Jermyn said, as the priest sank into the chair opposite him. He didn't think

133

he wanted to talk about magic to Eben, especially not with Duncan around. Or did he? Maybe Eben would be a good person to ask about local rituals and superstitions—the village priest ought to know about them, if anyone did. "You look like you've been working hard."

"I have," Eben said, pouring himself a cup. "Every year it seems Solstice preparations start earlier and last longer. I don't know why the winter festival wears me out so."

"*Because* it's winter, maybe," Jermyn offered. "Midsummer and spring, the celebrations are all outdoors. And the autumn pageant is so much a part of harvest that it doesn't feel like extra. At least that's what my aunt says," he finished shyly.

"Your aunt is a perceptive woman," Eben said, helping himself to a biscuit. "I hear from Duncan that Mother is recovering well."

"Yes, sir, she is," Jermyn said. "She's resting now, though. She promised Brianne."

"That's good." Eben looked pensive. "You'd know, wouldn't you? From what Duncan said about the accident, I'd guess that the master-to-journeyman connection is beginning to establish itself between you and Mother. So you should be able to tell if she's exerting herself, even at this distance."

"Maybe not at this distance," Jermyn temporized. The link stretching from him to Lady Jean was personal, and he found that talking about it made him uncomfortable.

"Perhaps not." Eben sipped tea. "I seem to remember that it takes from several months to a year for a journeyman to take hold fully. Doesn't it?"

"It depends," Jermyn said, not committing himself to anything. "Everyone is different."

"Well, congratulations on your progress, in any case," Eben said, smiling. "And if it helps Mother, so much the better. By the way, what were you and Maudie Mattock discussing when I came into the kitchen?"

"Um, not much," Jermyn said. "She asked me if I wanted fresh tea."

"I didn't realize you'd met," Eben said, frowning. "She isn't the sort of person I'd think you'd be interested in."

"Because she's a hedgewitch?" Jermyn asked. "But Mistress Allons said she isn't—isn't a problem to the Wizards' Guild."

"I know Mother's opinion of the matter," Eben said stiffly. "She and Maudie grew up together—ah, you didn't know that? It's true, though Maudie is the younger, believe it or not. Her father was one of the grooms up at the Tower when Mother was a girl."

"You think Mistress Allons is being too soft on Maudie?" Astonishing, to think of Lady Jean as older than Maudie. "But the Guild—"

"The Guild followed Mother's recommendation, as the master wizard in place," Eben said, sighing. "No, I don't think that Mother's wrong. As village priest, however, I could wish Maudie were —not so tolerated. Especially when she meddles in religious matters. Hedgewitchery can be perilously close to the black arts. And my parishioners *will* go to her instead of coming to me for their souls' welfare, or going to Jemima for their bodies' healing. I try to stop them, but. . . ." He spread his hands wide, indicating helplessness.

"I see," Jermyn said slowly. *Maybe I won't ask about local rituals. He sounds as if he'd hate the very idea of such a thing. I'd better wait and see what Mistress Allons thinks. I should be able to show her the memory of what I sensed, now that we're linked. And I'm going to have to talk to her about Maudie soon anyway.* "You don't think Maudie has any true talent, then."

"If she did, she would have entered the Guild," Eben pointed out, sounding very logical.

Maybe, Jermyn thought. It was what he had believed, once, himself. Now, he wasn't so certain. He was beginning to think that there were some kinds of power the Guild didn't recognize. Or, at least, didn't have any use for. Out loud, he said only, "I suppose so."

"In any case, how *did* you meet her?" Eben asked.

"Brianne introduced us," Jermyn answered absently; then he caught himself. *Oops, I don't think I should have said that.*

"Brianne visits Maudie?" Eben said, disturbed. "I didn't know that."

"Not *visits,* exactly," Jermyn said, alarmed. He certainly didn't want to tell on Brianne by *accident.* "Delia and I had gone for a walk in the woods and—uh—met her. Them. Look, don't tell Brianne's father, will you? I don't think he'd like it."

"No, he wouldn't," Eben said. "Does Mother know?"

"She knows about Maudie, of course," Jermyn said, unwilling to admit that he hadn't yet discussed the matter with his journeyman-master. "She said Maudie isn't a problem, I told you that. And she—Lady Jean, I mean—she's been pretty weak since the accident with the crystal. She rests a lot. If Duncan gets upset, he'll just make things worse." He paused, wondering if he'd said enough or too much.

Before he could decide, there was a crash and the sound of rending wood from the church. "What's that?" he asked, startled.

Eben jerked to his feet. "The scaffold!" He plunged out of the kitchen.

Jermyn followed, shoving his way through the kitchen workers in his urgency.

In the church, a woman screamed—a high, shrill sound. The scaffold was swaying where it stood, one side ripped loose and bending, the other starting to collapse in on itself.

"Brace it!" a man's voice shouted. "Brace it! The center'll hold long 'nough!"

Long enough for what? Jermyn wondered. *Why don't they just get out of the way and let it fall?* He elbowed his way to the front and saw why. Trapped underneath the collapsing scaffold, Brianne and Jemima stood very still. Brianne was white and shaking; she clung to Jemima, who had an arm around her shoulders.

"Hold quiet, miss an' ma'am," Sig Cammy said, from outside the mess. "We'll get you out a'there."

"What happened?" Eben asked, beside him. Duncan Campbell was standing next to him, rigid.

"It just—gave way," he said to his brother-in-law. "The bracing snapped."

"Rotten," said a man Jermyn didn't know, shaking his head. "Rotten boards. Ought t'use stone footings—"

Sig Cammy turned on him. "Wood was sound, I tell ye! I planed it mysel'. It just went over, soon as the women got in there."

"Never mind that now," Eben said. "We've got to get them clear before the whole thing collapses. Sig, can you—"

The platform creaked, tilting forward, toward the floor. Jemima patted Brianne's arm mechanically, and they both looked fearfully up at the heavy mass over their heads. One of the men shouted again as the left side of the heavy logs bent under the strain of holding the whole load.

It's going to go, Jermyn thought. *Any second now. And there's nothing anyone else can do about it in time—*

Slowly, he raised his hands. The bright gold cord of the familiar-link pulsed, drowning out all the other colors in his mind. *Je'm'n?* Delia said, her mind-voice puzzled. He could almost smell the warm, moist air of the conservatory through her nostrils. *Trouble, Je'm'n?*

Trouble, Dee, he told her. Power swelled all over the little church. Mistress Allons had forbidden him to work magic on his own, and the one thing he'd tried had turned into a disaster, but this would be a disaster anyway if he didn't do something to prevent it. His hands traced the outline of a shield spell in the air in front of him. *I need your help.*

Here, Je'm'n, she said trustingly. *Make good magic.* Strength poured through her into him, drawn from the air and sun and sky around them—more than enough for what he had to do.

I'm indoors, he reminded himself, struggling to remember his best version of the spell. *The air sign won't be too strong—the earth sign is strong enough—there. I can do this. If I hold it that way, just over their heads. . . .*

Magic flowed through him, out through his

fingertips. A rainbow arc of magic lit up the dim church interior, twisting lazily in the air in front of him. It ignored the wood of the collapsed scaffolding, sliding around and through, to cover with an open bowl, the female forms crouched underneath. Delia hummed in the back of his head; he reached for more strength, thickening and reinforcing the shield. *Nice and easy—that's it—*

The scaffold gave way with a great splintering roar, scattering the crowd. Duncan Campbell cried out in anguish. Standing perfectly still, his eyes closed, Jermyn concentrated his whole being on the twin poles of the curved shield and his link to his familiar. *Balance—hold the balance—*

"Jermyn!" Someone was shouting at him, taking him by the shoulders and shaking. "Jermyn, let it go! They're safe! Let the shield drop!"

There was a wrench in his mind, a ripping pain shooting through him. Delia hissed, but even her anger couldn't break through the whirling confusion in his mind. He had a sudden, totally bewildering glimpse of Lady Jean's white face.

"Jermyn!" Duncan howled again.

"Yes, all right," he said. With a relief that was more than physical, he released the spell. The magic brightened briefly, then swirled into a multicolored mist and was gone.

8

THE PRICE OF MAGIC

JERMYN CLOSED his eyes, feeling the power flow away from him. The familiar-link pulsed briefly, and then Delia's presence in his mind was back to its usual touch. He breathed deeply, his head swimming.

That was strong, he realized.

Good Je'm'n, Delia said as her voice faded, her tone a mixture of pride and worry. *Good magic. Rest.*

All right, he said. *I will. . . .*

When he could see clearly again, the first thing he saw was Brianne's face. She was sitting across from him on a pile of spare lumber off to one side of the church benches, her eyes wide and wondering. Duncan was next to her, dabbing ineffectually with his kerchief at a shallow cut on her cheek. She reached one hand out tentatively, then drew it back.

"Jermyn?" she asked. "Are you all right?"

"I'm fine," he said, trying to mean it.

"I'll be the judge of that," Jemima said from beside him.

"Jemima!" Jermyn said, reminded of the healer by her own voice. "Are you hurt?"

He twisted his head to look around, and he gasped as a wave of weakness assailed him. Clinging to the boards under him with both hands, he fought to stay conscious. Then a pair of strong hands pushed him back upright.

"I'm right here," Jemima said. Her healer's hands ran quickly over his forehead, pressing gently all the way down to his shoulder. "Sit still for a minute while I check you over. Hmm. Nothing much wrong with you except reaction. Been a while since you've done Primary Power sorcery, I should say. Right?"

"Right," Jermyn said. He didn't mention that an extraordinary occasion early in his apprenticeship had been the only other time he'd *ever* done it.

"All you need is rest, then," she said. "I've people hurt physically—cut and bruised by all the junk that was flying around in here. You just sit there and catch your breath while I go tend to them. Fair enough?"

"No problem," he said, nodding. Pain shot through his head, and he grimaced.

"Headache?" Jemima said, looking sympathetic. "I shouldn't wonder. I'll have one of the women fix you a cup of willow tea. You really should learn to pace yourself, you know. Magic isn't free."

She stopped to check on Brianne and say a few soft words to Duncan, then she strode off. Jermyn leaned back against the church wall, glad enough to sit still.

Brianne was still looking at him, her expression almost awed. "I've never seen anyone work magic like that before," she said softly. "I didn't know anyone could."

"Your grandmother could, once," Duncan said, his voice as quiet as hers. Jermyn couldn't read his face. "Annalise—your mother used to watch her for hours. . . ."

So this is what it means to be a spellmaker, Jermyn thought, as if it were a wholly new and unfamiliar idea. *The spell wasn't—isn't—very good yet. It still wouldn't be safe outdoors. But it's my spell. I made it and I controlled it. I could hand it over to another wizard for casting, if I wanted to. I've never felt that level of conscious control before—or that level of power.*

"Are you sure you're all right?" Duncan asked gruffly, not even looking at Jermyn.

"I'm sure," Jermyn answered, clearing his throat. "Just tired. Like Jemima said, magic isn't free. I'll be as good as new in a few minutes."

Brianne looked worried. "Father told me that Gran always had to take time to recover, but I thought that was just because she was old."

"Any magic requires energy," her father said, his jaw tightening.

I wonder what he's remembering, Jermyn thought. *Something about his wife, I bet.*

Duncan continued, "Experienced wizards usually minimize the effect, but even they can exhaust themselves if they are taken by surprise."

"I've seen it, myself," Jermyn said, agreeing with him. "Especially in wizards who've been working a Great Magic."

"That wasn't a Great Magic," Duncan said sharply.

Jermyn frowned. "Of course not. You need at least one master for sorcery at that level, and better two or three. Most Great Magics are worked in concert."

"I know that," Duncan said, his eyes boring into Jermyn. Brianne looked at him questioningly. "I was trying to find out if *you* did."

"You could just ask," Jermyn said shortly. *As if I'd even* think *I could work a Great Magic by myself! Well—be fair. He's had a scare, and he doesn't like magic. He probably isn't thinking too clearly right now. I know I'm not.*

Jermyn closed his eyes with a sigh. Around him, the noise of men working swirled. He could sense Jemima's healing magics flickering throughout the room as she applied her abilities. *She's good*, he realized. *As good as Healer Collins back in the city. She could almost be a master healer. I wonder why she isn't?*

There was something else, too, niggling at the edge of his mind—like something he could almost remember but couldn't quite put a name or a face to. He almost had it. . . .

Eben's voice jerked him out of his musing. "Are you all right?" he said, his voice as harsh as Duncan's had been.

Jermyn opened his eyes. "Didn't Jemima tell you I was?"

"She did, but I wanted to see for myself," he said, pushing a hand through his untidy hair. "Brianne, sweet, are you much hurt?"

"I'm fine, Uncle Eben," she said, smiling at him. She wiggled the fingers of both hands in his direction. "See? Just a few bruises. No broken bones."

"You ought to be home in bed," Duncan said. "We should leave—"

"Wait a minute, if you don't mind," Jemima said, coming up behind them. "I'd like to beg a ride, if I could, and I really shouldn't leave just yet."

She handed Jermyn a cup of willow tea. "Thanks," he said, gratefully sipping the bitter brew. "My head's pounding like someone is driving nails into it."

"You're lucky it isn't worse," Eben said. "Do you realize how dangerous that was?"

"I realized the dangers," Jermyn said, grimacing slightly. "I just didn't think I had much choice, is all."

"What ever made you try earth magic without a proper grounding?" Eben went on, as if Jermyn hadn't spoken. "If your control had slipped, even a fraction—"

"I was grounded," Jermyn said, beginning to be angry himself. *First Duncan and now Eben—does everyone think I'm an idiot?* "I know better than to work unlinked. I wouldn't have had nearly enough power if I hadn't been drawing it through my familiar."

"You can't have been focusing properly," Eben insisted. "Your familiar is all the way back at the tower."

"I can reach Delia from here well enough," Jermyn said. "We've got a pretty strong bond. Maybe I couldn't have done something complicated, but grounding is basic. And my control *didn't* slip."

Eben still looked grim; Jemima intervened. "That's enough, Eben. I don't want my patient scolded anymore until he's had a chance to recover. Except by his healer, of course, and I've already done all the scolding I'm going to do today. Because I, for one, am very glad that he took the risk he did. If he hadn't, both Brianne and I—well, we might have survived having that platform land on our heads, but it wouldn't have been pretty. And since I *am* the only healer around these parts, we probably wouldn't have had much chance to recover afterward."

"That's true," Eben said, looking shaken. "But when I think what might have happened—"

"Never mind," Jemima said. "Just be thankful it *wasn't* worse."

"I am," Eben said. "I've never liked the winter Solstice platform. It is always too narrow and tall for a structure made of green wood."

"It wasn't the wood," Jermyn said slowly, as the scene around the scaffold came back into focus. "At least, I don't think it was. There was something else. . . ."

"Right you be, Young Master," Sig Cammy said, at his elbow. His face glistened under the bald head; he looked like an outraged gnome. "T'wood were fine. Look a' this."

He held out two flat pieces of wood, the ends

neatly sheared in a diagonal cut. Eben took them and turned them in his hands curiously.

"That's an odd shape for lumber," Duncan said, frowning.

" 'Tis plain foolish," the carpenter said indignantly. "And I'll be Powers-taken-below if *I* ever cut a piece o' good wood into suchlike line. It was right where the bracings give way, Reverend."

"But—what happened to it?" Jemima asked, sounding puzzled.

"Old Maudie says 'tis bad spirits," Sig said, his voice hushed.

"Now, that kind of talk I will not have," Eben said sharply. "You tell Maudie that I tolerate her in church for the sake of her daughter's family, but if she's going to make irresponsible statements like that she won't be welcome anymore."

"But it was magic," Jermyn said, reaching out to take the board. He ran his fingers along the cut edge carefully, half-afraid he would feel heat. "Here, and here—see?"

"I do," Jemima said. She placed one hand on the piece of wood without taking it from Jermyn. "There is a shadow of a spell on the wood, though I can't sense anything very clearly. Sig, did you use any of your construction spells today?"

"Well, uh. . . ." The carpenter positively shuffled in embarrassment. He didn't look at Eben. "Not today. But y'know, Reverend, 'tisn't easy to get the

148

wood cut and planed for a scaffold just so quick, in winter. An' snow came early this year, and there was Squire Poncebry's new shearing shed to finish before the frost set in too deep. . . ."

"So you used magic to prepare the wood, after I expressly asked you not to," Eben said, his jaw tightening. "I knew I should have checked on you."

"You asked me not to build t'platform with binding spells, for fear they'd interfere wi' t'Solstice Rites," Sig protested. "Ye didn't say nowt about seasonin' t'wood."

"But how could magic go wrong to make the boards break like that?" Brianne asked, sounding interested. Beside her, Duncan looked black, but he didn't say anything.

"Only magic *could* make boards break so evenly," Jermyn told her, running his fingers along the broken side. "Look, it's cut right across the grain—I don't think you could get it that smooth with a saw. I suppose an old working spell could have reversed, if it hadn't been checked in a while. Then it would have weakened the wood instead of strengthening or seasoning it. I can't tell for sure, though. The magic's fading too fast."

"That does it," Eben said, taking the board and tossing it aside. "From now on we'll be having the pageant on the ground, as I've been arguing we should for the past several years."

"Oh, hey, now, Reverend," Sig said, alarmed.

"Won't take but a moment to put a new lift up. Won't be as high, maybe, but 'tis better off t'flooring."

Around him were mutters of agreement from the villagers—even from the man who'd wanted stone footings, Jermyn was amused to note. Eben looked exasperated.

"It will take hours of hard labor and you know it!" he said. The mutterings deepened, and he threw up his hands in mock surrender. "All right, all right. I know when I'm beaten. If you want to work the night solid and on into the morning, who am I to stop you? I just wish some of you had shown this much energy last summer, when we were trying to get the new roof put on the chapel before the rains came."

A ripple of relieved laughter went through the crowd as it started to disperse. Eben turned back to Jermyn.

"Since you and Jemima did pick up a hint of witchery on that board, I need to ask you something," he said, the grimness back. "Do you think there is any chance that our local hedgewitch is involved?"

"Eben, don't be silly," Jemima said. Next to her father, Brianne bit her lip and glanced nervously at Jermyn. "I know you don't like Maudie, but she isn't capable of something like this."

"I'm not so certain of that," Eben said. "Jermyn?"

"It could be, I suppose," he answered, avoiding Brianne's eyes. "She—I thought there was something in the kitchen right after I was talking to her, but I'm not sure what. Everything happened so fast. . . ."

Eben nodded. "It did indeed. Which leads me to my next question." He looked sternly at his niece. "Brianne, my dear, just *how* well do you know old Maudie?"

"What?" Duncan asked, startled. "What do you mean?"

"It's a legitimate question, Duncan," Eben told him. "Or were you aware that your daughter has been visiting Maudie Mattock?"

"I asked you not to tell him that!" Jermyn protested.

Ignoring Jermyn, Duncan rounded on his daughter. "Brianne, is this true?"

She lifted her head. "You're always telling me that I'm supposed to visit the sick and old, so I do. Why not Maudie?"

"Because she's a hedgewitch, that's why!" her father roared. "You—"

"Duncan, be quiet," Jemima said sharply. She nodded at the interested faces all around them. "You're making a scene. Eben, can't this wait for some privacy?"

"Perhaps you're right," he said heavily. "Very well. We'll talk later, then, Duncan. Brianne, I'm sorry. Jermyn, forgive me for breaking a confidence, but I felt that Brianne's father should know about her activities."

"Certainly I should," Duncan said, glancing accusingly at Jermyn. Unlike Eben, he didn't respond directly to Jemima's suggestion, but he did lower his voice. "I should have been told immediately. Brianne, is there anything else that you haven't been telling me?"

Brianne shook her head, pressing her lips together as if daring a word to slip out.

"I didn't tell you because Mistress Allons said that Maudie wasn't malicious," Jermyn said, more to support Brianne than to defend Maudie. Or even himself. "Mistress Allons wouldn't—"

He froze, his hands clenching suddenly into fists.

"Jermyn, what's wrong?" Jemima said, concerned. "Is it a backlash? If the magic hasn't dissipated properly, it might be affecting you."

"No—no," he managed to get out, opening and closing his palms. "Not me. Not here. Mistress Allons—she—"

Once he'd said her name, it was as if a mist had cleared from his mind. The thing he'd been trying to remember was Lady Jean's face, glimpsed through a rent torn in the magic as he was releasing the spell. The memory had returned urgently, demanding that he take action—now, at once.

"Grandmother?" Brianne said. "Do you mean she's the trouble?"

"Nonsense!" Duncan said, his voice firm. "Don't be ridiculous."

Jermyn looked at them without seeing them. "She's *in* trouble. We've got to get back to the Tower!"

Duncan wanted to ask more questions, but Jermyn wouldn't be denied. Brianne backed him.

"If something is wrong with Gran, we've got to get to her right away," she declared. "What if she's sick or—or if she's fallen and hurt herself? There's no one at home but the servants, and they wouldn't go into the workroom unless she called them."

"They will this time," Duncan said firmly, though he was clearly shaken. "I left orders that someone was to check on her regularly."

"What if she's locked the door?" Brianne said. "She often does. Jermyn?"

"I don't know," he told her helplessly, feeling only the beat of panic. "I just know we've got to get back."

"Then I think we should all go," Eben said, looking disturbed. "Don't waste time, Duncan. The sooner we go, the sooner we find out."

"I'm going with you," Jemima said grimly. "If Jean is ill, you'll be sending for me anyway."

Duncan had come in the carriage, driving it himself; they took that because it was larger, and they left the sleigh in the village.

Sitting by a window with his arms wrapped around his body, Jermyn tried to hide the shudders that racked him. He knew he was being irrational, but he didn't care. He wanted to scream at Duncan to drive faster, to push the horses as hard as they could go. *Whatever is wrong, is terrible*, he thought numbly. *Whatever it is, I've got to get back. Get there. Now!*

After an eternity, the carriage pulled up under the covered entrance. Jermyn was out of the door and into the house almost before the horses had come to a full stop. One of the maids, dustmop in hand, faced him open-mouthed.

"Young Master!"

"Out of the way," he said, pushing past her to the stairs. He took them two at a time, heading for the workroom.

He could hear steps behind him on the stairs. Brianne called to him to wait, but he didn't pause.

"Mistress," he gasped, wrenching open the workroom door, "is anything the matter with—"

The sight inside stopped him as if he'd been turned to stone. He couldn't move—couldn't think. Brianne screamed, pounding on his back, but even then he didn't move until Duncan or Eben forced him out of the way.

Lady Jean was sprawled on the carpet, her face pale and her eyes closed. Her full skirts of blue brocade spilled across the floor in front of the hearth; one arm was stretched over her head, while the other one twisted beneath her body at an unnatural angle. Beside her, the broken fragment of the crystal glowed blood red in the firelight.

The Spellmaker was dead.

9

FUNERAL

E BEN KNELT beside the body, and began to pray in a ragged voice. Jermyn paid no attention. Cold gathered around his heart, isolating him. He couldn't think, couldn't even cry out. His mind remained empty, except for one sentence constantly repeated.

I killed her. My magic—my wonderful control. I killed her.

He knew that was how it had happened, even before Jemima bent to touch the body with careful fingers.

"Sorcery," she said in surprise. "It's confusing, but she reeks of it."

Lady Jean's body reeked of Jermyn's shield-spell. When he'd released his hold on the spell, instead of dissipating evenly, it had followed the line of journeyman-master link to Lady Jean. The backlash had killed her.

"She must have realized what was happening," he said numbly. "Our link was so new, she might not have been expecting it any more than I was, but she would have recognized a spell backlash. Only she wasn't strong enough to fight it. That's why—she must have gone to the crystal to try to call for help. If it hadn't been broken. . . ."

"Even if it hadn't been broken, who would have heard her?" Eben said from beside the body. His face was gray. By the door, Brianne wept in her father's arms. "You and Jemima were otherwise occupied, and there is no one else in Land's End who is capable of hearing such a call."

His words washed over Jermyn in a rush of air; they didn't seem to touch him. Nothing could change what he had done.

I killed her. It's all my fault.

He had felt guilt like this before—when Aunt Merry had fought with Fulke the Weather Wizard for his sake, when she'd become ill with the sorcerer's plague that had almost destroyed the entire

Guild. But this was worse. His own actions had killed Lady Jean. Brianne's grandmother. Master Eschar's friend.

Adding to his guilt was the feeling that he hadn't exactly been close to Lady Jean, not as close as he was to Master Eschar. And by disobeying a direct order of hers—*work no magic without my permission*—he had killed her.

Eben tried to comfort Jermyn, but he had his own load of guilt to bear. "I should have made peace with her years ago," he kept saying. "What was so important that we had to stay apart so long?"

It was Duncan who took charge, which dimly surprised Jermyn. Somber and controlled, he ordered his mother-in-law's body carried to Tower Landing's chapel at once.

"We'll have the funeral here, if you don't mind, Eben," he said, once the servants had removed their silent burden. "And the vigil as well. I know it's customary to go down to the village, but Mother wanted to be buried in the family crypt, below the chapel. It will be easier."

Eben nodded. "Yes, of course. Thank goodness we don't have to try to dig a grave in this frozen ground. I'll come up day after tomorrow to make the arrangements. And someone should notify the Wizards' Guild—Jemima?"

"Certainly," she said. "I can use my own crystal for that much."

Jermyn wondered distantly what the Solstice pageant would be like in Land's End this year. It would have to go on. The Church required it, and too many people were involved. But it would obviously go on without the participation of the Allons family. Except for Eben, who had to be there. *Poor Eben.*

Poor Brianne.

Poor all of us.

Days passed. Jermyn lived through them without noticing. He ate mechanically; he washed, dressed, and spoke when spoken to; he even remembered to fold his clothing and tidy his room. All of it required about as much effort and conscious thought as breathing.

Delia never left him, even to eat. Duncan had glanced at her sharply when she followed him into the dining room the first time, but Brianne set a dish on the floor without comment, and her father had held his peace. For that, Jermyn was grateful. He wanted desperately to talk to Aunt Merry or Master Eschar, but he couldn't. Jemima's crystal was tuned by special spell to her healing talent, and he couldn't ask to borrow it after what had happened the last time he'd used someone else's crystal. He even thought about writing a letter, but mail was so irregular in winter that it hardly seemed worth the effort.

Instead, he spent most of his time in his room or in the library. If he kept a book open in front of him, people tended to leave him alone. That was why he was staring at Kates's *On the Art of Spellmaking* on the morning of Lady Jean's funeral.

Some art, he thought bitterly. *All it does is kill. At least in my hands.*

Brianne opened the door and closed it quietly behind her. Delia, sitting on Jermyn's lap, squeaked a greeting. Jermyn did not look up.

She sat down across the table from him. "Good morning. What are you reading?"

"Good morning," he said politely. "Nothing."

"Doesn't look like nothing to me." She bent her head to look at the cover; obligingly, he lifted the book so she could read the spine. "Umm. Isn't that one of the rare books from the workroom?"

"Yes, but I'd been leaving it down here to read," he said, idly flipping pages. "Anyway, your father asked me to put all the workroom books into the library. He thinks they'll be easier to catalog and take care of if they're all in one place."

"I suppose he's right," she said. When he didn't respond, she went on in a gentle voice. "Jermyn, you've got to stop this."

"What do you mean?" he said. "I'm just trying to figure out if this one goes in 'Thaumaturgics' or if I should start a special 'Rare Books' section."

"I don't mean reading," she said, slapping the book down on the table. "Or even pretending to read. I mean this—this blaming yourself."

He set his jaw and forced himself to meet her eyes. "Who else should I blame?" he said, his voice harsh in his own ears. Delia nuzzled him urgently, but he ignored her. "I killed her. Me, my spell, no one and nothing else."

"You also saved Jemima's life and mine in the process," she reminded him. "Had you forgotten that?"

"Of course not," he said. "But if I'd done it right, Lady Jean wouldn't have died. I was in contact with Delia—the spell shouldn't have backlashed like that. Or if I hadn't broken the crystal, we might not have been linked by magic yet. Or she might have been able to call for help—"

"Call who?" Brianne asked, as her uncle had before her. "While we're parceling out blame, why not include everyone? If your aunt hadn't been worried about you, you wouldn't have used the crystal in the first place. If Sig's spell hadn't gone off, the platform wouldn't have fallen. If I hadn't asked you to come with me to the village, you wouldn't have been there to save us. Would that have been better? For that matter, why did I have to go to the village in the first place? If I hadn't, Gran wouldn't have died."

She was crying, fat tears sliding down her cheeks. Jermyn stared at her, shocked out of his own misery. Tentatively, he put out a hand. "Brianne, please . . . please, don't cry."

"I'll cry if I want to," she said, through a glaze of defiant tears. "She was my grandmother, and I loved her, and it's my *right* to cry."

She buried her head in her arms. Jermyn set Delia on the table and circled around to pat one heaving shoulder. Tears pricked his own eyes, and he fought to hold them back. "I'm sorry. Here—do you have a kerchief? Take mine, Aunt Merry is always telling me to carry one. . . ."

She took the square of white linen from him and blew her nose. The gesture was somehow even more touching than the tears. "I'm sorry. It's just been so awful. Everywhere I look, I see her—it's like she's still here. And Father's invited the whole province to the funeral. Well, I suppose he had to, lots of them are mentioned in the will so they'll need to be here for that. But they have to be fed, and Cook's upset because rats have been getting into the grain again, and it's all just too much!"

She put her head down on the table. Delia sniffed it and touched her cheek with a cold nose.

She sad, she told Jermyn soberly. *Tired.*

"Uh-huh, I know," he answered aloud.

"What?" Brianne said, looking at him.

"I was just talking to Delia," he told her. "She says you're sad and tired."

Brianne leaned back in the straight chair and managed a half smile. She offered Delia a hand, then scratched lightly under the pointed chin when it was accepted. "Thanks, Dee. You've got more sense than most people."

"I just didn't think about what it was like for you," Jermyn apologized humbly. "I'm sorry."

She sniffed, wiping her eyes. "No one is thinking, not even me. Otherwise I'd be hiding in here with you."

He tried to smile—not very successfully, but he tried. "No, you wouldn't. You don't hide. You do things. Is there anything *I* can do?"

"Well, you can come to the funeral," she said, standing. "And the reception afterward, for the reading of the will. You'll have to come to that. Everyone does."

"All right," he said. "I'll be there."

"And, um . . ." She looked at the table a little guiltily. "It might be a good idea if Delia stayed out of sight for a while. I know she doesn't want to leave you, but after the last time—well. . . ."

"Delia will understand," he said. "Didn't you say something about rats getting into the grain again? That will give her something to do during the funeral, and after."

163

"It'll make Cook happy, too," she said, shaking out her skirts. For the first time, he noticed that she was wearing a black silk dress, slightly too large for her. It made her look pale and thin. "You'd better start dressing now. Uncle Eben will be here any moment."

He didn't have a black tunic, he'd discovered when he pawed through his clothes the day before. He wasn't sure he'd ever owned one; Aunt Merovice selected most of his clothes, and she liked bright colors. Delia trotted after him from wardrobe to dresser to water closet as he donned his compromise choice, a navy blue tunic with gray trim and dark leggings. It would have to do.

Anyway, I'm not family, he thought, brushing his hair in the mirror. *It wouldn't be proper for me to wear deep mourning. I wonder where Brianne got that black dress? It can't be hers—she looks like an old lady in it. Maybe it was her mother's. Or—*the steady rhythm of brush strokes faltered—*maybe her grandmother's.*

He took Delia down to the kitchen himself, by the back way, so he didn't risk running into any guests. Cook was busy preparing for the guests who would stay for a bite to eat after the funeral, but she spared Jermyn a nod and assurances that his familiar would be welcome. She also offered him a cup of tea and a sticky bun, since she didn't think he'd eaten much breakfast. He refused, saying he wasn't hungry. It was true.

Leaving the warm friendliness of the kitchen was difficult, but there were noises of arrival from the front hall. The chapel was half filled already. He slipped into the back as quietly as he could, hoping to hide himself in the crowd, but as he entered Eben caught his eyes and motioned him forward.

"Jermyn," he said in a low voice, "I'm glad to see you. Brianne wasn't sure you'd come."

"Of course I've come," he said, uncomfortably aware of the small silence that had fallen behind him. "I should have come before, for the vigil."

Eben shrugged. "Don't worry. I wasn't there for most of it myself. Would you mind sitting up front with the family today? There are so few of us—I asked Jemima to sit there, too. I have to be at the altar, naturally, and I think Brianne and Duncan could use the support."

Jermyn glanced up quickly, to see a somber Jemima seated in the front row. She flashed him a quick, encouraging nod, and he nodded back.

"All right," he said. "If you want me to."

The funeral was endless. Jermyn sat between Jemima and Brianne, with Duncan stony-faced at the end of the pew. Eben kept the service as brief as possible, from the moment when six villagers carried in the wooden coffin to the final invocation to the Powers Above for mercy and the Powers Below for rebirth. The worst part was following the coffin into the crypt. The twisting stone stairway was too narrow for crowds, so only the family and the pallbearers went down. And Jermyn, with Brianne beside him and Jemima just behind. Lady Jean was laid to rest in a crypt along the outer wall, one she had chosen for herself. The stone effigy of the original occupant—the long-dead-and-dust wife of one of her ancestors—was propped up alongside the open niche; it slid back into place with a scraping of rock.

Jermyn wanted to cry out as the coffin disappeared from sight. Brianne clutched his hand as if it were a lifeline—she was as cold as he felt. He noticed Jemima looking anxiously along the line of mourners to Duncan. All of this emotional pain must have been driving her Healing sense mad with the desire to help, but she wouldn't even try, Jermyn knew. According to the Healers' Guild, grief was something better lived through than artificially eased. Jermyn thought the Healers' Guild had too many rules, sometimes.

They left a covered lantern burning in the crypt as a dead-light, its soft blue radiance intended to comfort mourners coming for visits later. As he followed Eben up the narrow stairs, Jermyn was seized with a desire to go back and light more lamps, hundreds of them, to dispel the shadows lurking in every corner of the musty crypt. One small lantern seemed little enough to light Lady Jean's way into the afterlife.

Food was set out on a long table in the parlor, across from the hearth where Lady Jean had sat during the tea party. Chairs were organized for the reading of the will at one end of the room. Little groups of people clustered here and there; Jermyn recognized the Kestrells and Lydia Poncebry. He didn't see Reginald.

As the family party entered, the buzz of conversation paused briefly, then picked up again. Duncan guided Brianne to the front of the room, where Eben was already chatting gravely to a stout, white-haired man with round spectacles.

"That's Kennet Oldcastle, Jean's lawyer," Jemima said, taking Jermyn by the arm. "Come talk to my parents."

Jermyn hesitated, watching Brianne, who stood like a sleepwalker in between Eben and her father. He couldn't help her now, except by staying out of the way. And Mr. and Mrs. Kestrell's sympathy was like a hearth fire to warm a cold heart.

It wasn't until he had been talking to the Kestrells for a while that he realized that Jemima might have been trying to protect as well as comfort him. More than one covert glance from around the room was directed at him. *They're all looking at me*, he realized dully. *They must be thinking about how I killed her. Talking about it.*

Mrs. Kestrell kept up a flood of small talk that filled all the silences. Obviously, she understood the meaning of all the sidelong glances. ". . . Such a lovely sunny day, too. I always like days in midwinter to be sunny. They're so short, you know. It hardly seems fair for them to be overcast as well. Though my maid Ellen was saying this morning that we should be looking for another storm."

"Oh, there's Reginald," her husband said when she paused to take a breath. "I was wondering where he was."

Jermyn looked up to see Lord Poncebry in the doorway. The older man caught his glance, raised one eyebrow, and deliberately turned away. Jermyn flushed.

"Don't worry," Mrs. Kestrell said, squeezing his arm. "They just don't know any better, Jemima says. Look, Lawyer Oldcastle is calling for us. He must be ready for the—the reading."

Brianne settled into a chair in the front row, between Eben and Duncan. Her face was still fixed, but her hands twisted nervously in her lap. Oldcastle leaned over to pat her shoulder, and she flinched as if his touch were red hot. Jermyn frowned. *She's about to break*, he thought. *She's just holding on, waiting for the end. I hope Jemima notices.*

"Suppose we'd better be sitting down," Mr. Kestrell said. "Where's Jemima? She said she wants us to sit by her."

Mrs. Kestrell looked at Jermyn anxiously, but he managed to hang back as the assembled company found places among the chairs. This time, he was able to sit in a back row, close to the door.

Lawyer Oldcastle had a high tenor voice, not at all consistent with his round face and solid appearance. Before starting, he cleared his throat once or twice and finally coughed for silence. The company quieted.

"Well, now," he said. "I suppose we all know what we're here for."

The crowd murmured agreement.

"Get on with it, Oldcastle," Duncan said tightly. From where he sat Jermyn could see him try to take Brianne's hand, but she had them both clenched in her lap.

"Yes, yes, certainly," the lawyer said, ruffling his papers nervously. "Well. As some of you know, I've been—I was Lady Jean's man of law for several years. Ever since my father retired, in fact; and he was her father's man of law, once upon a time. In addition, as Justice for the Province, I think I'm fit to swear before the assembled company that what I am about to read is in fact and in deed the last will and testament of Lady Jean Allons. Are there any dissenters?"

"Of course not, Kennet," Eben Allons said wearily. He passed his hand over his face. "We all know that you wouldn't be party to any misconduct."

"I just wanted to be sure," Oldcastle said severely. "One must do these things according to form, after all."

"Oldcastle . . ." Duncan said, a threatening note in his voice.

The lawyer spoke swiftly. "Here we are, then. This document was dictated by Lady Jean Allons and written by me on the twelfth day of the second month, precisely twelve years ago. There have been only a few changes since. It begins: 'I, Jean Allons, being of elderly body and reasonably sound mind' —I told her that the phrasing wasn't customary for a legal testament, but she insisted—'being of elderly body and reasonably sound mind, do bequeath my worldly goods as follows. . . .' "

To judge by reactions, Jermyn thought, the disposition of property surprised few people. The servants received varying bequests, greater or lesser, while Duncan received a life tenancy in the tower, along with a respectable sum of money. The bulk of the estate was to be held in trust for Brianne, "until she come of age or choose to marry with her father's consent, whichever she may do first." To her only son, Eben, Lady Jean willed a sum of money exactly equal to that which she had left Duncan, "hereinafter to be held in trust for a Priest of the Church." That drew some knowing glances around the room, as the listeners reminded themselves of the estrangement between Lady Jean and her son. One or two people looked disapproving. Jermyn noticed Lord Poncebry in particular shaking his head. Poncebry himself received a strip of land "along the northern border of the Foxkin Woods, so that he may stop worrying about the beavers damming the stream on my side"; and Jemima Kestrell received the contents of Lady Jean's herbarium and such plants from the conservatory as she had a use for and felt able to tend properly—"Phineas Mayhew will know the best to transplant."

In addition to the main inheritance, Brianne received a large sum of money separately, "to be used for her education, or as she sees fit," Lawyer Oldcastle said disapprovingly.

"When she comes of age?" Duncan asked in surprise.

"No," Oldcastle said. "Now—at once, if she desires to leave Land's End to attend school. I am instructed to make all the necessary arrangements, according to her own wishes in the matter."

Duncan's mouth fell open; he looked stunned. Brianne started to weep again, as she had in the library, great gasping sobs that tore at the air. She buried her face in her hands. Jemima stood up hurriedly and went to her, putting an arm around her shoulders until the sobbing eased.

So Lady Jean did mean her granddaughter to become a wizard, if she wanted to, Jermyn thought, surprised that he wasn't more surprised. *At least, she made sure that Brianne could make her own decisions. I wonder why she waited so long? Well, maybe she just didn't feel up to fighting Duncan directly. Or maybe she just couldn't bear to send Brianne away.*

At the front of the room, Duncan's expression was thunderous. He glared at Jemima and the weeping Brianne, opening his mouth to say something, but Eben caught his arm and whispered urgently in his ear. Then Jermyn saw the healer jerk her head meaningfully at the crowded room, already beginning to buzz with conjecture, and Brianne's father subsided.

He nodded tightly at Lawyer Oldcastle. "Very well. Let's finish it."

Oldcastle adjusted his spectacles. "There is only one more item," he said. " 'Finally, I leave the contents of my library—to be understood as those books in my workroom and those which are stored in the tower library proper and excepting only those volumes which have personal application to my family, here listed—to William Eschar, Master

Theoretician, to do with as he pleases in his lifetime and after."

"What?" Duncan said, jerking upright. "She can't do that—some of those books have been in the family for generations."

"Calm down, Duncan," Eben said. "She probably kept the family books separate, Kennet? Didn't you say something about a list of exceptions?"

"I—ah—did so," the lawyer said fussily. "However, I must inform you that the list of volumes excluded from this bequest includes only such books as pertain to the Allons family genealogy, and a few personal papers."

"That's ridiculous!" Duncan stormed. He sounded relieved to have an obviously neutral reason to shout. "Those books are *valuable*. Why, only last winter, she spent a third of the wool revenues on manuscripts."

"I did advise Lady Jean of the size of the bequest," Oldcastle said stiffly. "Several times. I felt it was my duty to do so."

"And I'll bet you got exactly nowhere with your advice," Eben said, with a rueful smile. Oldcastle pursed his mouth. "It does seem—oh, well. Come on, Duncan, don't be a fool. Eschar is a distinguished scholar, with an Empire-wide reputation. No doubt Mother felt he would make better use of the books than you or I. Or Brianne," he said, smiling down at her more wholeheartedly. "The valuable part of the library is largely books on sorcery, isn't it? Well, then."

"A great estate should have a library," Duncan snapped, unwilling to let go of his grievance. "It isn't appropriate—"

Brianne looked up from Jemima's shoulder, sniffing slightly. "Uncle Eben is right, Father," she said, reaching out to touch his arm tentatively. "Don't—don't fuss. Please."

Her father looked down at her, his expression strained. He took her hand and laced it tightly between both of his; Jermyn could see the muscles tense from halfway across the room. "Brianne. . . ."

Oldcastle cleared his throat again, meaningfully. "If you *don't* mind, Mr. Campbell, I have not quite finished with the bequest," he said. "There is a recent codicil, dating from this winter—sixteen days past, to be precise."

"A codicil?" Eben said. "What could that be?"

Oldcastle lifted the page and read precisely: " 'The contents of my library, as herein stated, are to be left to Master William Eschar during his lifetime, with the understanding that he may do with them as he pleases—both adding and subtracting from the collection as he sees fit,' " the lawyer intoned portentously. " 'Upon the death of Master Eschar, the collection, in whatever condition he has left it, is to pass into the possession of Journeyman

Spellmaker Jermyn Graves, to do with in his turn as he sees fit.' "

Jermyn felt his mouth fall open in shock; several people twisted in their chairs to look at him.

" 'In addition, my communications crystal—to be understood as the Orianhri-cut crystal normally kept in my workroom—is to be given into the possession of Journeyman Graves immediately upon my death,' " Oldcastle finished dryly. "That is all. Further details concern the fate of the library should Journeyman Graves predecease Master Eschar. They are unimportant at this time—"

"The crystal, too?" Eben said, startled.

"Journeyman Graves!" Duncan said, springing to his feet. He shook off his brother-in-law's arm. "But he broke the crystal in the first place!"

Eben frowned. "I'm sure Mother didn't know that would happen when she wrote the codicil. Duncan, please—"

Duncan shook off his restraining arm. "No, Eben, I will not be quiet. You can't say that—that sprat is a distinguished scholar. He's a tradesman's son, with no more hope of gathering such an expensive collection of books than I have of becoming Ruling Prince of the Empire. And the crystal—even broken, it's an heirloom. It belongs in the family."

Jermyn found himself on his feet too. "I don't want the books, or the crystal. I never asked—she never said anything to me about *any* of this."

"Not likely," a voice in the crowd muttered. Jermyn thought it was Poncebry, but he couldn't be sure. "So that's why he did it. . . ."

A horrified hush settled over the gathering.

They think I did it on purpose! They think. . . . Jermyn swayed, stunned. *I have to get* out *of here.*

He couldn't breathe; he pulled at the collar of his tunic and gasped for air. At the front of the room, Brianne reached out to him.

"Jermyn, wait," she cried. "Father didn't really mean it."

Jemima was already moving purposefully toward him, fumbling in the small healer's case that she'd discreetly carried in a skirt pocket.

"No!" Jermyn said again, louder. "I didn't. I *didn't!*"

He stumbled backward, overturning a chair. He had to get away from this room, from the forest of staring eyes and clutching hands that would have held him back. Delia chittered angrily in his mind, furious as she realized that he was leaving her; but he couldn't wait. He grabbed a cloak from the pile in the front hall and swung it over his shoulders; there were shouts behind him, but he paid no attention. He had to get to open air. He had to breathe.

Then he was outside, running alone under the pale blue sky and weak sun of midwinter.

10

EARTH MAGIC

JERMYN RAN into the woods, struggling through branches and high underbrush; the thick snow underfoot made him flounder. He stumbled more than once, only to push himself up and start running blindly again. Hot tears scalded his face, and his breath came in gasps. Finally he fell headlong into a thicket and lay there, panting and sobbing with exertion.

Burrowing under the dead branches, he cried, wailing like a small child. Gradually, the sobs gave way to hiccups. In the end, he fell into a deep, exhausted sleep, his face pillowed uncomfortably against the brambles.

It was Delia who finally recalled him to himself, pushing her nose into the hand that lay clenched across his chest.

Je'm'n? she said worriedly. *Je'm'n cold.*

He roused reluctantly, struggling into a sitting position and blinking at the afternoon shadows. "Dee? How did you get here?"

Je'm'n cold, she said firmly, and climbed into his lap to curl against him. *M'here.*

"Yes, you are," he said. He hugged her tightly to him, burying his face into her snow-streaked fur and feeling very sorry for himself. "Oh, Dee, I wish we'd never left home. I wish I'd never been born!"

Silly, she said, nuzzling him. *Silly Je'm'n.*

He sniffled, rubbing the back of his hand across his eyes. "I guess I was pretty silly, running away like that. Falling asleep in the snow is a good way to freeze to death. It's just all so awful. I wish—I feel so alone."

He wanted Aunt Merry, but he didn't want to say so. Even to Delia. Somewhere, in the back of his mind, he knew that he was acting like a child—and a small, scared child, too—but he couldn't seem to help it.

Delia understood. *Both here,* she told him, nuzzling him again. *Not alone.*

"Yes, you're here, too," he said, ruffling her fur.

He took a deep breath: time to start acting his age. "I almost forgot. I'm sorry, Dee. I'm being silly again. No more, I promise."

No more silly, she said, agreeing with him. After one more nuzzle she hopped down from his lap to look up at him commandingly. *Go?*

He smiled reluctantly. "Yes, ma'am. Whatever you say."

He stood up, brushing off the borrowed cloak as best he could. At least the dark tunic he'd put on for the funeral was warm—and at least he'd had sense enough or luck enough to collapse in the sun. *They say the Powers take care of wise men and fools*, he thought, disgustedly taking stock of his condition. *I know which I've been today.*

"Do you know how to get home?" he asked his familiar, embarrassed to realize that he had no clear idea of how far he'd come, or in what direction.

Uh-huh, she said, frisking a little around his feet. *That way.*

"Then we'd better get moving," he said with a sigh. He didn't want to go back to Tower Landing—didn't want to face Duncan, or Eben, or even Brianne. But he didn't have much choice: the shadows were already lengthening into evening.

They had gone perhaps a third of the way through the woods—Jermyn was starting to think he recognized the path—when Delia suddenly stopped and snuffled along the ground.

"What's the matter?" he asked sharply. "What do you smell?"

Funny smell, she said, in confusion. *Funny bad smell*.

"Magic?"

Uh-huh.

He looked around. "We aren't far from that hedgewitch's hut. Do you think that might be it? Like last time?"

Like, not-like, she said, still stiff with concern.

Jermyn considered. The last time Delia had sensed the hedgewitch's sorcery in the woods, she'd been intrigued and curious but not upset. This time, of course, she had had an upsetting day. *We both have*. Still, she sounded serious. He extended his own senses, trying to share in hers. She let him in willingly, but all he could feel was a sort of confused, strange *wrongness*, as if something were out of place or off balance. Not like in the church or at the tea party, exactly—this was tangled and twisted, but looser. It was more like the natural thicket of the woods around him than any orderly magic.

Funny, Delia repeated, clearly troubled. Frustrated, he stopped probing; that wasn't getting him anywhere. Whatever was out there was beyond the reach of his senses, both physical and magical.

I'd better take a look, he decided finally. "All right, then. Let's follow your nose."

But the trail led them straight to Maudie's hut. Jermyn hesitated at the edge of the clearing, the sense of *wrongness* growing in him. Delia stirred uneasily on the ground, instinctively taking up the position of a skunk facing a challenge: feet planted firmly, tail ready to lift. The hut was inhabited— he could see smoke curling from the stone chimney—so Maudie must be home. There was no other sign of life, not even the dog.

What is *it?* he asked himself, rubbing the back of his neck with one cold hand. *Dee's right—it's like and not-like it was before, and I don't like the smell of it at all.*

Bad, Delia said sternly from beside him. She hissed softly, in warning. *Not-good.*

"That's the definition of 'bad,' all right," he said. "I guess we have to find out just how bad this is."

He rapped lightly on the door of the hut. At least Maudie might let him warm his hands at her fire before she chased him away. She might even offer him a cup of tea. He was so bone-cold, he wouldn't even care if it tasted buttery.

It wasn't Maudie who opened the door. It was Brianne.

"Jermyn," she said, an unreadable variety of expressions chasing themselves across her face. She took a deep breath and seemed to settle on feeling relieved. "Oh, thank goodness. Maudie said—but I didn't—where have you been? I—that is, we've been worried about you, Father and Uncle Eben and I."

"I can imagine," he said shortly, unpleasantly aware that his face was streaked with tears and his eyes puffy and red. Maybe she'd think it was all due to the cold; he could hope. But that wasn't being fair to Brianne. She probably *had* been worried. "What are you doing here? Where's Maudie?"

"I—uh, that is. . . ." She almost moved to block the door, but it was too late. He had already seen Maudie behind her, poking up the hearth fire with a charred stick.

"Great," he said in disgust. "Terrific. Brianne, is this really the right time for a magic lesson?"

Her mouth fell open. "How could you think I'd be so irresponsible? I'm not—oh, never mind. You'd better come in and get warm."

"If you aren't having a lesson, then what are you doing here?" Jermyn asked, following her. He almost sighed with relief as the heat from the fire hit him; even Delia seemed happy to be warm again. "I greet you, Mistress," he said to Maudie.

The hedgewitch nodded at him, pursing her lips

with faint satisfaction. "'Bout time you got here," she said.

"What?" Jermyn was confused for a second, then he noticed the crude circle sketched on the hard-packed dirt floor, the wooden bowl of water on the room's one table—and the lacy white shawl draped across it. He knew that shawl. He'd seen Lady Jean wear it. "Brianne! What are you *doing?*"

"We're going to do a Questing," Brianne said, lifting her chin defensively. "That's when you call up the spirit of the dead to answer questions. Maudie's going to work the spell and I'm going to hold the opposite side of the circle for her. Maudie knows how. Don't you, Maudie?"

"Aye, aye," the old woman said, shuffling over to the table. "Better with three, it is. The old ways, the earth's ways—clay not long in the ground, dust not yet to dust. Maudie knows, Maudie knows. Call the earth—"

Jermyn stared, speechless for a moment. He didn't understand everything the hedgewitch had said, but he understood enough. Delia pressed shivering against his ankles. "You're going to Summon the spirit of the dead? That's black art!"

"We aren't going to do any such thing," Brianne said furiously. "I wouldn't think of it. This is a Questing, not a Summoning. It doesn't command. Jermyn, nothing in Guild law prohibits asking questions. I swear, I checked. I even asked Uncle Eben."

"You told your uncle you were going to do this?" he said, even more startled.

"No, of course not," she said impatiently. "He thought I was asking about the kinds of things the authorities might do to investigate Gran's death. Only he said even a wizard competent in the Spirit Calling technique would have to try it as soon as possible after the—after the death, and that by the time such a wizard got to Land's End, it would be too late. He didn't think of Maudie."

"And you did," Jermyn said, putting his hands on his hips to look at her. He glanced at Maudie and lowered his voice to a furious whisper. "Of all the crack-brained schemes—do you know how dangerous what you're planning is? You'll be working awfully close to a Great Magic. Worse, you're going to try to do it with one elderly, untrained hedgewitch and her sort-of-apprentice. You're crazy!"

"Maudie knows how," she said stubbornly. She glanced at the old woman for support, but the hedgewitch only snorted without looking up. "She's done it before. We've got the bowl, and the herbs, and Gran's shawl to use as a focus—"

"If Maudie's done it before, she ought to know that you can't draw a circle of magic with only two people," he pointed out. It was easier to argue with Brianne than the hedgewitch—and if he could get Brianne to agree, there would be no need to argue with Maudie. "It takes three points to make a circle. That's elementary geometry."

"Maudie did say that three of us would be better," she admitted. "But I overruled her. You can make a circle with two points, if you have a compass. Or a good eye."

"Do you *have* a compass?" he said scornfully. "You don't have time to practice. Do you even know what the magical equivalent of a compass *is?*"

"Well, what is it?" Brianne said. "If you're so smart—"

He sighed and ran one hand through his damp hair. "A thing of Power, preferably belonging to a third wizard, one not present in the circle. Your aunt's crystal would do, even broken. You use the object to trace the circle."

"Oh." For a moment, she looked abashed. Then she recovered. "Maudie's got her scrying-stone. Maybe that will do. Or no, you said it had to be from someone not present in the circle. Well, we'll manage."

"Brianne—"

"Look, if you're so worried about how dangerous this is, why don't you help?" she challenged him. "I told Maudie you wouldn't, but you could. You're a journeyman. You could be the third point on the circle. And I'd think you'd want to find out the truth about Gran's death more than most."

He felt his face grow stiff. Maudie looked up

from her preparations, finally, to chuckle at him. "Eh, young 'un? You afeerd what we may learn?"

He started to deny the implications fiercely, but Brianne forestalled him. "Of course he isn't. Jermyn, I'm sorry. I didn't mean—I just meant that you were Gran's student, her last journeyman. Don't you owe her memory something?"

"I know the truth," he said heavily. "So do you. I lost control of my spell-release, and it killed her."

"That's just plain silly," she said, lifting her chin at him. "Whatever happened, it couldn't have been that simple. Gran was old, but she wasn't crippled. She must have done something—fallen asleep, miscalculated, *something*. And not what all these awful rumors are saying. Maybe she was trying to repair the crystal herself when—when the backlash happened. Whatever it was, we have to find out."

He studied her in silence. She was leaning forward, face flushed and eyes intent. Her sandy blond hair, pulled back in a loose braid and wound roughly around her head, made a golden halo in the firelight.

"You really want to do this, don't you," he said quietly.

"I have to," she answered simply. "Father wants to contest the will."

"What?" Jermyn was startled. "He can't think —on what grounds?"

"Undue influence, because of that final codicil about you," she told him. "The rumors gave him the idea, I think. I heard him arguing with Uncle Eben and Jemima about it after everyone left this afternoon. He says Gran was old and ill and didn't know what she was doing."

"That's ridiculous," Jermyn said scornfully. "Mistress Allons always knew exactly what she was doing, even at the end."

"Of course the bequest to you is only an excuse," she said starkly. "Oh, Jermyn, don't you see? It's because of me that he wants to get the will set aside, if he can. The extra bequest to me has him so—so furious and scared, he can't see straight."

He saw. Duncan wouldn't be happy to have his daughter slip beyond his control—able to study magic by her own choice if she wished. *Maybe he thinks if he can hold her back long enough, she'll change her mind. Or maybe he just* isn't *thinking.* "What does your uncle say?"

She rubbed her face in her hands. "Uncle Eben says that you've been acting a little oddly but he's sure it isn't anything to do with the inheritance. He won't admit that you aren't really the point. Jemima says that Father is making a fool of himself and he'll eventually come to his senses, but I can't bear it. Gran left me that money for my education. Now that I know what she meant by telling me to be patient, now that I have a chance, I have to know for sure how she died—especially if it was by magic, like my mother. Somehow, I have to convince Father that Gran was right in doing what she did, and this is the only thing I can think of that might help."

"It might do just the opposite, you know," he warned her soberly. "If your grandmother did die from just the spell-backlash, it might convince your father that the dangers are worse than he's ever imagined."

She shook her head. "There can't be anything worse than what he already believes. The truth has to be better. A little better, at least."

He looked down at Delia, sitting by his feet. *Dee?*

Magic, Je'm'n? she said doubtfully. *Funny smell. I know. Can we do it?*

Her head tilted as she considered Brianne thoughtfully. *Yes, Je'm'n. Yes-yes. Je'm'n do, not bad.*

"Oh, that's just wonderful," he said aloud. Brianne looked at him questioningly. "My familiar has informed me that if I help, what you're going to do won't be black art. I guess my presence will keep you on the right side of the Powers or something. That's just *great*."

The hedgewitch chuckled again, shaking her head as if she couldn't believe her own ears. "Fool boy," she said amiably. "City boy. 'Bout time you faced up to it."

Brianne smiled slightly but didn't look away from Jermyn. "Then you will help?"

"Do I have a choice?" He shrugged out of his cloak. "Tell me what do and where to sit."

Maudie put him on the side of the circle away from the fire. "North," she told him seriously. Her country accent had almost disappeared. "North's male, and so's you. Listen to what the land speaks to you." She took the southeast side for herself and placed Brianne to the southwest. The wooden bowl of pure water—melted snow, Brianne told him— she placed in the center of the table, with the shawl unfolded beneath it. She sat with her eyes closed and bent her head over her clasped hands, between which rested a blue-gray stone about the size of a man's palm, very smooth with polishing.

Without opening her eyes, she nodded at Brianne. "Begin."

Brianne took out a small leather pouch, shiny with use, and dribbled black powder out of it around the bowl, so that the powder made a rough circle on the material of the shawl. Jermyn eyed it narrowly, soothing Delia in his lap with a stroking hand. The powder looked like coal dust, with maybe some sort of bark ground in. It was a mixture he'd never seen before.

Master Eschar should be here, he realized, trying to take mental notes of everything. *He loves finding out about new magic rituals, even primitive ones.*

Especially primitive ones, maybe, because they're so seldom written down.

Maudie lifted her head and howled, the long thin sound raising the hair on the back of Jermyn's neck. Delia hissed.

"Aieee!" the old woman cried, lifting the stone between her hands. "Water and Earth, be near, be near!"

Jermyn stared in astonishment as the stone floated in the air over the bowl of water, then descended into the exact center of it without making a ripple on its surface. He'd known Maudie had some talent, but he hadn't realized how much. *That's real power!* He braced himself as she howled again.

"Aieee! Fire and Air, be near, be near!" A spark appeared out of nowhere and raced around the circle that Brianne had laid on the cloth. As it passed Jermyn, he felt a twisted cord of magic slip into his mind, touching him and binding him into the circle. It was a rough, jagged cord, with peaks and valleys like the flame burning on the table. Instinctively, he sought to steady it.

Water and Earth, Fire and Air—she's inverted the standard invocation, he thought. Then Brianne entered the circle of magic, and he forgot everything else.

Brianne had a magical talent, all right. Pure, bright power burned from her, the soft greens and browns of springtime. Her presence in the circle was like a warm, soft wind, bringing life back to the dead lands of winter. He knew that touch; he'd felt it before.

A healer, he thought, when he could think coherently again. *Brianne's a healer. Why didn't Jemima see it? Why didn't Mistress Allons?*

He knew the answer to that, too, when he thought about it. The healing art was one of the most difficult to identify. So many people had a touch of it, in some form or another, and so few had enough to be useful. Like spellmaking, healing was a form of earth magic. The test for healing powers always involved an actual invocation of Earth in the presence of the potential apprentice healer. Which might mean that Maudie's gift was also some form of earth magic too, since she'd made the invocation.

He looked at the old woman, straining every sense. *Yes—yes, it is. I can feel the pull of the earth in her now. Maybe being a hedgewitch, living as she does in Earth's shadow, has something to do with it. She isn't strong enough to waken Brianne's gift alone, but she can do it with me here to help. And it's only Brianne's presence, with her awakened gift and her kinship with Lady Jean, that makes this a—what did she call it?—a Questing, not a Summoning*, he realized. *This way, it isn't black art. Otherwise, it might have been. Did Maudie know that?*

The circle of fire smoldered on the table. Jermyn

forced his attention back to the spell. White-faced and trembling, Brianne reached out to either side, and Jermyn and Maudie each took one of her hands. Then Jermyn forced himself to hold out a hand to touch the hedgewitch—physical touch would finish the spell, she had said.

Their hands met. A spark of pain shot up Jermyn's arm. He didn't think he cried out, but Brianne did.

"Grandmother!" she cried, her voice agonized, eyes wide and fierce. "Grandmother, please!"

The water in the bowl—or maybe it was the stone in the water—started to glow. The light was a rich red-gold that grew brighter until it was painful to look at. Jermyn turned away, then made himself turn back. Maudie's eyes were open but blank; he didn't think she was seeing anything.

The light flickered, turning silver at the edges. A mist glittering like shards of glass caught in smoke rose from the center. Slowly, it gained height and thickness, extending up from the center of the table to the thatch of the hut. Features formed, made out of flames and smoke. Jermyn stared. *It's too strong! It shouldn't be so powerful. That can't be—*

Jean Allons. Herself. Her soul.

Her presence filled the air and darkness. She was younger than he'd known her, about the age of the portrait in the parlor, but her features—the high cheekbones, the wide-set blue eyes, the arched brows so like Brianne's—were unmistakable. She was wearing the blue dress she had worn the day she died, and the shawl that they'd used as a focus. Her hair, barely touched with silver, streamed in red-gold waves down her shoulders. She lifted translucent hands imploringly across the circle; her mouth moved, but no words came out.

Then, like a blown-out candle, she was gone.

11

SILENCE

JERMYN was too stunned even to be frightened. "Powers Above and Below," he whispered. "What was *that*?"

"It was a ghost." Brianne's face was as pale as smoke. "Gran's spirit. Uncle Eben says—"

"Aye," Maudie said, rocking back and forth on her stool. "When the dead come whole for t'calling, 'tis a bad, bad thing."

"Oh, I know it was a ghost," Jermyn said. He pulled his hands away to stroke Delia, who was trembling. "But that was far too vivid and solid to be an ordinary revenant."

"That was my grandmother," Brianne cried, her voice rising. Suddenly she seemed very near tears. "Her—her essence, her very self—I could feel it."

"So could I," Jermyn said quietly, thinking back. There were still echoes of that impossible presence in his mind. He could almost hear the whisper of Lady Jean's skirts sweeping the dirt floor of the hut. "But if we managed to call her, she must have wanted to come. She must be near. . . ."

"Of course she wanted to come," Brianne said. "She knows—we never had a chance to say goodbye."

"No, Brianne," he told her. "Think. It's got to be more than that. There's only one way your grandmother could have come to us as—as completely as she did. And that's if she didn't die naturally."

Brianne gave a little whimper and closed her eyes, swaying. For a moment, Jermyn thought she was going to faint.

"You're saying she was killed on purpose, with magic," she whispered. "Killed by someone who wished her ill, who intended her to die. Powers of Earth, Water, Air, and Fire—Jermyn, who? Who could have hated Gran so much, to kill her with black art?"

"I don't know," Jermyn said slowly, drawing in a deep breath. "But *I* didn't kill her. It wasn't my spell after all. . . ." The wave of relief that washed over him as he said the words out loud was so powerful that it threatened to overwhelm him. An hour earlier, he would have been shouting the news until the woods rang with it; now he had to push it aside. He was free, but at what price? *I didn't kill her—but someone did.*

Who?

The obvious answer occurred to him at once. Standing slowly, he turned toward Maudie. The old woman watched him intently.

"Jermyn, we've got to tell them," Brianne was saying urgently. "We've got to tell Father and Uncle Eben that it was murder."

"We do," he agreed. He didn't add, *Your father is going to be furious;* that was understood. "And maybe we have more than that to tell him."

Brianne frowned. "What do you mean?"

Jermyn hesitated, then plunged ahead. He spoke directly to the old woman. "Mistress Maudlin Mattock, in the name of the Guild of Wizards and of all the Powers, I charge you—did you think that you were working the black art today, with Brianne and with me for your tools? What do you know of the death of Mistress Allons?"

"Eh?" The hedgewitch tilted her head at him. Her eyes narrowed slightly, and he thought he saw the shadow of alarm in her expression. "What's that you say?"

"Jermyn, no," Brianne said, taken aback. "Maudie wouldn't have hurt Gran."

"Well, here we have a murder done by magic, which is black art," Jermyn told her, swallowing. "And here we *also* have an unlicensed magic-worker. It's just a little suspicious, don't you think? Your uncle doesn't trust her, I know that much. I'm pretty sure the Guild will want to question her once we—"

"No," Maudie said, interrupting him. The hedgewitch's hands were clenched in the front of her ragged dress. "Ye'll not tell. Not *him*."

"We have to—" Jermyn started to say, and then her spell caught him by the throat.

Brianne cried out. "Maudie, what are you do-ing?"

"No!" the hedgewitch said, spreading her arms wide and pointing at him. "Ye'll tell Priest, an' he'll—an' wizards'll come fra the city—they won't listen to old Maudie. They'll listen to you, if you thinks—but no one listens to old Maudie. No one cares about her. Terrible big place the city is, Maudie's been there oncet. Not goin' back. Not goin' in a cell, a stone box, a grave for t'living— not!"

Jermyn staggered backward, tripping over Delia. The skunk hissed, vibrating in her rage. She set her feet firmly, started to stamp—but this was no physical attack to be warded off by bad odors. Maudie's magic was crude and disorganized, but she struck through the connection they had all three made in setting up the Questing.

Jermyn had no defense against it. He heard Brianne scream, saw her hands go to her own throat as she gasped for breath. Then the world went dark.

When he woke, the hut was dim; the hearth fire had almost burned down. Delia was a warm weight on his chest. Her eyes gleamed at him anxiously as she butted her nose against his chin. Automatically he reached up to scratch her head.

Dee? What happened?

Je'm'n! Her squeal was as good as the words. *Je'm'n wake up. Wake up–wake up.*

"I'm awake. I'm awake," he said, groaning as he tried to sit up. Whatever Maudie had thrown at him, it made him ache all over. "Where's Brianne?"

"Here," said a breathless voice from the other side of the table. "Maudie's gone, and she took Gran's shawl with her."

Jermyn sniffed. "No, I think she burned it."

Brianne was pale and shaky, but she pulled herself to her feet and righted a fallen stool to sit on. "We'll never find her—she knows these woods better than the Poncebry huntsman. What did she *do?*"

"I'm not sure," Jermyn admitted. If he squinted, he could see a soft swirl of transparent magic in the air around Brianne. No doubt he had a similar swirl around himself, where he couldn't see it.

"You look strange," Brianne remarked. "Sort of—double."

"That's the spell, I think," he said, reaching for a stool for himself. He had to pull himself up on it while Delia anxiously tried to climb his leg. The interior of the hut was still spinning. "Yes, yes, I'm all right, Dee. Just give me a minute."

"Spell?" Brianne asked. "What sort of spell?"

"I think it's called a Silence," Jermyn said. "I've never seen one before, so I can't be sure. You put it on someone when you don't want him to talk about something."

She went even paler. "Maudie wouldn't—she—you mean, she doesn't want us to talk about—to talk about Gran being m-m-m—"

She stopped, unable to breathe around the stuttering, her eyes wide.

"Yes," Jermyn said grimly. He already knew better than to try to talk about Lady Jean's death. When Brianne tried, brown haze thickened around her until she was almost covered with it. "I told you she was involved."

"And *I* told *you* that she wasn't," Brianne said. Her voice gathered strength as she spoke. "I don't believe it."

"Then why did she make a Silence? Why did she run?" Jermyn asked. "It isn't that I want to think she's guilty. But nothing else makes sense."

"It can't be," Brianne told him firmly. "She must have run because you threatened her with the Guild, the way Uncle Eben always does. It couldn't have been Maudie, Jermyn. Why would she help me by doing the Questing if she was involved in Gran's death?"

"I hadn't thought of that," he admitted. "But hedgewitchery can be close to black art, even your uncle knows that, and so was Maudie's Questing. If I hadn't been here to awaken your healing talent—"

"What?" Brianne's mouth fell open as she stared at him. "What did you say?"

"You're a healer, like Jemima," he said. "I spotted it as soon as Maudie finished the invocation. That's how they test healers, by invoking an earth magic, and you responded right away. Only Maudie doesn't have enough strength to awaken your gift on her own. If I hadn't been here, it wouldn't have happened. And without your gift and your blood tie to Mistress Allons, that spell would have been pure black art."

"A healer." Distracted, Brianne was awed and wondering. "I'm a healer. Are you sure? Oh, Jermyn. . . ."

"I'm sure," he said, nodding. He would have

grinned at her amazement if the situation hadn't been so serious. "But do you see why I think Maudie might be a black artist? If she could take a chance like that, she could do anything."

"Not killing Gran," she said positively. "She *liked* Gran. Besides, Maudie kept asking for you today. She even wanted me to go and look for you. I didn't understand why, and she wouldn't really explain, but it does sound as if she knew she needed you to help. Doesn't it?"

"It does, sort of," he said, thinking back. "I suppose she could have recognized you for a healer through her own earthsense, and then decided to use my presence in the invocation to awaken you. Oh, . . . I don't know. If it wasn't Maudie, then who was it?"

They stared at each other for a few moments. Finally Jermyn shook off his paralysis. Reaching for his cloak, he said, "Well, we can't do anything here. Let's get back to the tower."

"Then what?" Brianne asked, picking up her own wrap. "Can you break the Silence spell?"

"I don't know," he admitted. "It looks pretty loose, but there's an awful lot of raw power behind it. Master Eschar always used to tell me that primitive doesn't mean weak, and I guess he was right. Maybe if we go to Jemima, she'll be able to see that something's wrong."

Brianne frowned. "What about Uncle Eben?

201

He's a priest—he's used to working with the Powers. Won't he be able to see something?"

"I don't think so," Jermyn said. Personally, he was betting on Jemima. "I think he'd have to be right in the middle of a ritual to notice anything. It all depends on what Maudie actually did."

The wind outside was biting and chill, the sun only a dim orange glow behind the trees. Jermyn shivered and put Delia on his shoulder. *Yes, I know we don't have your nice leather pad again*, he told her when she complained about not having a comfortable place to hold on. The suffocating pressure of the spell made him short with her. *I swear, I'm going to start lacing that pad on the moment I get up in the morning, just in case. And I swear I will never again underestimate the power of a hedgewitch.*

"Jermyn, what if Jemima can't tell that anything is wrong?" Brianne asked, her voice very small.

"Then we'll have to think of something else." *Will Jemima even be able to see the spell? Brianne and I can both see it, but we were present when it was cast.* "We won't find out standing around in the woods."

They trudged back to Tower Landing single file, Brianne giving Jermyn directions and Jermyn breaking the path. Delia clung to Jermyn's shoulder, her claws digging painfully through his clothing, but he didn't scold her; she was upset enough. Maudie's spell bothered her—she kept trying to bite through it, as if it were a cloth she could help him cut, and then recoiling in distaste from the oily wisps of magic. *Is it black art?* Jermyn thought to himself. *It's got to be earth magic, at least. What does Maudie want from us, anyway? If she isn't guilty, then why did she run?*

It was full dark by the time they reached the tower, only to find it ablaze with light and bustling with people. Brianne clutched at Jermyn's arm. "What's going on? Do you think—?"

She stopped talking as the spell took hold. He shrugged, the magic silencing him as well. But a brief hope stirred in his own heart. If Jemima had discovered that something was wrong with Lady Jean's death—or if Eben had begun to suspect something —then maybe. . . .

But the torches and the noise were not for Jemima. Or Eben. Ranged around the foundations of the tower was a troop of men in the uniforms of the Royal Guard. As Jermyn gaped at the unexpected sight, an even more surprising figure walked around the front of a sledge: Felix Morrenthau, Master Spellcaster of the Guild and head of the Council of Wizards. Behind him was—

"Master Eschar!" Jermyn cried, his knees almost giving way in a sudden excess of gratitude and relief. "How did you get here?"

"Overland, by the mail road," the Theoretician said crisply. Lines of weariness were deeply graven into his lean face. His eyes were sunken with exhaustion. "And a filthily uncomfortable trip it was, too, every step of the way. Jermyn, what in the name of the Empire is going on?"

There wasn't much Jermyn could tell him. Duncan Campbell insisted that they meet in the front parlor, where the portrait of Lady Jean looked down on the room in disdainful majesty. Jermyn sat facing it, trying not to look up. He'd sent Delia to their rooms. She hadn't wanted to go, but her presence in the parlor would only have irritated Duncan. *Nothing serious is going to happen to me indoors,* he said to her sternly. *You can say hello to Master Eschar later.*

Huh, she said, flicking her tail at him as she started to hike herself up the stairs to the second floor. *Be good, Je'm'n. Call.*

I will, he promised. *Don't worry. I'll call right away if I need help.*

Eben told the story of his mother's death slowly but succinctly. Jermyn didn't really listen. He concentrated instead on trying to signal Master Eschar that something was wrong. Only it didn't seem to be working. Either Eschar was too tired to pay attention, or he had more important things on his mind than a former apprentice. Once Jermyn caught Spellcaster Morrenthau looking oddly at him and then at Brianne, and hope flared in him. The Master Spellcaster ought to be able to spot a Silence, if anyone could. But then Morrenthau looked away and the hope died.

"Yes, I understand the nature of the accident," Eschar said in his deep voice. He groped for his pipe with one hand and then—looking up at the portrait—stopped. Jermyn felt tears sting his eyelids. Mistress Allons had not permitted smoking in the house. "What I don't understand is the nature of the sorcery in question."

"Well, *I* don't understand why you are here," Duncan said, glaring.

"The death of any master wizard concerns the Guild," Morrenthau said, speaking for the first time. He was a thin man, short and slight, who had only been head of the Council of Wizards since the death of old Steen Douglas. Eschar said that no doubt he'd grow into his position, given time. Merovice Graves found him annoying, and even Jermyn had thought he was awfully pompous the few times they'd met. "We set out as soon as I received the message from your healer. When the Master Spellmaker—the only Master Spellmaker in the Guild—dies suddenly, the Guild investigates."

"But to travel so far north at this time of year is risky," Eben said, frowning. "And by the over-land route. You're fortunate you made it."

"We had a good team of men with us, and a good guide in the mail rider," Eschar said. "A local man—perhaps you know him? Rene Cammy."

"Oh, yes, Sig's elder brother," Eben said, nodding. "He's a fine tracker, but still you took a chance."

Eschar sighed, rubbing the back of his neck. "We had no choice. As my honorable colleague has indicated, when the Master Spellmaker dies, the Guild takes action. Actually, I've been more or less expecting trouble ever since Merovice—Mistress Graves—told us how Jean's crystal broke."

"Aunt Merry!" Jermyn blurted out. "I didn't know she was still in the link when the crystal broke. Was she hurt?"

"She's fine," Eschar said, smiling slightly. "She even wanted to come with us."

"It would have been most inappropriate," Mor-renthau said disapprovingly. "We have no need for an herbalist."

"Yes, well, I'm not so sure of that," Eschar said. "This region has a limited number of Guild wizards of any sort, and Merovice works well with healers. We'll have a hard time finding a competent pathologist this far north."

"Pathologist?" Duncan said, his eyes bright with suspicion. "Why will you need a pathologist?"

"When a master wizard dies unexpectedly, there are always suspicions," Morrenthau said portentously.

"We do have to be certain of precisely *how* she died," Eschar said gently. "Just in case."

Eben looked worried. "Oh, but surely—my mother was an elderly woman, not strong. An accident could quite easily have carried her off."

"I disagree," Duncan said, looking at Jermyn meaningfully. "I think you'd be wise to investigate *every* possibility."

Jermyn opened his mouth to defend himself. "I didn't," he choked out, but then the Silence took him by the throat and he gasped for air.

No one noticed except Brianne. She reached over and squeezed his arm, biting her lip helplessly.

"Brianne, you've had a long day," Duncan said, pulling her away from Jermyn. "You should go to bed."

"Yes, Father," she said, but she didn't move.

Eben was arguing with Master Morrenthau. "If you suspect something, you must have a reason. Why would anyone want to hurt Mother?"

"That is usually a simple enough question to answer," Master Eschar said calmly. "Who benefits from her death?"

Brianne went white, glancing wildly at Jermyn. He shook his head at her. *I benefit, Brianne benefits—even Master Eschar benefits, though he doesn't know it yet. Oh, if only I could get him alone, I know I could make him understand what's wrong.*

"You do, for one," Eben responded forthrightly. "Mother left you her library. We were all very surprised."

Eschar looked amused. "So she didn't tell you she was willing the books to me? Well, well. How secretive of her."

"You knew?" Duncan said. Even Eben looked taken aback.

Eschar shrugged. "More or less. We'd been arguing about it for years. I said she ought to give them to the Guild. How many did she leave me?"

"All of them," Eben said heavily. "Every blessed volume."

"Only for your lifetime," Duncan said, his eyes narrowing. "She left you the management, and—young Mr. Graves—the remainder when you were done with them."

The way he said "young Mr. Graves" was itself an accusation. Jermyn stared at Duncan angrily, waiting for Eschar to take him down a peg for his presumption, but the Theoretician only sighed.

"How well she knew me," he said, sounding rueful. "The collection will of course stay intact—I don't think I've ever been able to force myself to dispose of a book. Hmm. So she wanted Jermyn to have her library in the end, did she? That's interesting."

"*And* her crystal," Duncan said. "The crystal *he* broke."

"I didn't break the crystal!" Jermyn burst out. He was surprised that he was able to say it, but evidently that episode wasn't completely covered by the Silence.

"Who did, then?" Eschar asked crisply. "How did it break?"

"I—I don't know," Jermyn answered miserably, very conscious of all eyes upon him. "It just broke."

Morrenthau stared at him unforgivingly. "Really. In my experience, crystals do not 'just break.' You'll need do better than that—journeyman."

Jermyn swallowed, feeling trapped. How could he explain what he didn't understand? "Yes, sir. I'll—I'll try."

Duncan looked satisfied, like a cat that had just spotted a birdcage with its door open. Eben looked troubled, and Brianne was frankly appalled. She kept glancing back and forth between Master Eschar and Jermyn, her face drawn into deep, agonized lines.

"Well, we've had a long day," Eschar said when the pause had extended for what seemed like a hundred years. "What do you say, Morrenthau? Start fresh in the morning?"

The Spellcaster frowned. "We should talk to the healer who called us, as soon as possible—what's her name, Kestrell? And I'd like a look at that crystal tonight. I may be able to form some theories about the causes and consequences of the fracture."

"It's in the workroom," Jermyn said, leaning forward eagerly. *This could be my chance*, he thought. *If I can get Master Eschar alone in the workroom—or even him and the Spellcaster—I can at least give him a hint.* "I can show you just how it happened—"

"Journeyman Graves is not to be included in the investigation," Duncan said sharply. He looked at Brianne as if he were wishing she'd left the room, then went on doggedly. "I won't have it."

Eschar raised his eyebrows. "Of course not. It wouldn't be proper."

Jermyn blinked, confused.

"Really, Campbell!" Morrenthau went stiff in outrage. "Mistress Allons was a respected member of the Wizard's Guild. You can trust us to deal with her death appropriately. Journeyman Graves will assuredly not be a part of the ongoing investigation—not until his own involvement is clarified."

"That isn't enough," Duncan said. "I want him placed under guard."

"What?" Jermyn straightened. "But I didn't—I haven't *done* anything."

"Father, don't be silly," Brianne said. She stopped, struggled over the choice of words, and then rushed into speech. "Jermyn isn't—isn't going to run away. Where would he run to?"

"Brianne, be quiet," Duncan said, looking away from his daughter. "I am the master in this house now. Spellcaster Morrenthau, I must insist. The village constabulary is small, but it has the appropriate facilities."

"It has one cell," Brianne said scornfully. "With two bars missing and a lock so rusted that a child could break it."

"I would say that your father makes sense, child," Eben said. He was staring at Jermyn with a strange expression on his face.

"But Jermyn wouldn't—he didn't—" Her sentence ground to a halt.

"Of course I have a point," Duncan snapped. "Eben, you said yourself that the boy has been acting strangely."

"I did, though I thought grief might account for most of it," Eben said. "However . . . Jermyn, just what have you been up to this afternoon?"

"N-nothing, sir," he managed to get out.

Eben shook his head. "I wish I could believe you, but there's a strong feeling of magic about both you and Brianne. I can't tell more than that, but— Master Morrenthau, do you see it?"

"Brianne!" Duncan went white. He wrapped one arm fiercely around her shoulders and turned to Jermyn. "What have you done to my daughter?"

"Nothing," Jermyn cried again, passionately.

"He didn't hurt me!" Brianne said, starting to cry—tears of frustration and rage this time, if Jermyn was any judge, but tears nonetheless.

Morrenthau was examining Jermyn intently. "Hmm. Yes, I do see something—wish I'd been able to bring my familiar. Eschar?"

"How would I see anything magical?" the Theoretician said irritably. He looked his former apprentice up and down critically. "It could be an aftereffect of some sort, I suppose. Theoretically speaking."

"It could," Morrenthau said, nodding. "We will have to investigate. In the meanwhile, Journeyman Graves, you will consider yourself confined to your rooms. Tower Landing is isolated enough that I think we can dispense with the cell in the village. However, all magical equipment will be removed from the premises—I will see to that myself. And there *will* be a guard on the door. Theoretician, do you agree? I ask you to respond in an official capacity as representative of the Wizards' Guild. We don't have a full circle, but we may as well do this formally."

"By all means," Eschar said, shrugging. He looked away from Jermyn, not meeting his eyes. "If you think a house arrest is necessary, I certainly won't object. Er—that is, in my official capacity as Master Theoretician representing the Guild, I agree with your actions, Guildmaster."

They can't think I'm guilty, Jermyn thought, the words of protest caught in his throat. *Can they? Duncan might, or Eben, but not Master Morrenthau—not the head of the Council of Wizards. Master Eschar wouldn't let him think I was guilty.* Master Eschar *wouldn't. . . .*

He looked helplessly at Brianne, who was sniffing furiously. Tears streaked her face. *Brianne believes in me. I can see it in her eyes.* He clung to that belief gratefully.

But there was a cold knot of fear growing inside of him.

12

HOUSE ARREST

Two guardsmen from the city troop escorted him to his rooms, looking very tall and splendid in their black uniforms. Jermyn felt like a child walking between them, but he tried to act adult and confident—like a journeyman wizard. Delia met him at the door. If he hadn't known that she was picking up on his own emotions, he would have thought she was angry with him.

Bad men, she scolded as he sank wearily down on the bed. *Bad men hurt Je'm'n. What do?*

"I don't think there's anything we can do," he said, pulling off his tunic. "Except get some rest."

She sent him a picture of Master Eschar, frowning as he did when he was worried about something, and the sense of a question. *Go see. Yes?*

No, he told her, not willing to say the thought out loud. Her sympathy eased his own hurt a little, and he forced himself to consider the matter more calmly. *He can't help us. Or he won't.*

There's nothing to worry about, he told himself as he dunked his head in the basin and tried to wash some sense back into it. *Look how Master Eschar already asked who might benefit from Mistress Allons's death. Brianne and I saw her ghost, and we didn't think of that. And Master Morrenthau—you don't get to be the head of the Council of Wizards by jumping to conclusions. They'll figure it all out.*

Won't they? Jermyn tried not to consider the alternative, but the chill in the pit of his stomach wouldn't let the idea go away. *If only we could have told Master Eschar about what happened at Maudie's. Or if only Eben or Master Morrenthau had been able to see Maudie's Silence for what it is, instead of just general magic. Maybe then Duncan wouldn't have pushed so hard and gotten me locked up like this.*

Or maybe Duncan would have pushed anyway. Maybe Duncan has a reason for accusing me. The possibility made him clench his teeth and swear as the water slopped out of the basin. *Duncan benefits. He didn't know that Mistress Allons was going to* leave that extra money to Brianne. And he could be pretending to hate magic, to hide his own talent—and his use of it.

Jermyn ticked off the supports. Duncan had been upset when Jermyn had come to study. *He might have known I'd spot something, like I did at the tea party or in the church.* Duncan hadn't wanted the rare books on magic or the broken crystal to go out of the family. *He might have a use for them himself.* Duncan didn't want Brianne to learn magic. *He might be planning to teach her himself, so he can dominate her gifts. Powers, what will it do to Brianne if it turns out that her father killed her grandmother?* Duncan's wife had died in a terrible magical accident. . . .

Jermyn clenched his fists reflexively on the sides of the basin, feeling sick. He startled Delia, who started sniffing quickly for enemies. "Don't worry, Dee," he reassured her, taking a deep breath and reaching for a towel. *I can't tell Brianne I suspect her father. Not without proof. She just wouldn't believe me—look how she was about Maudie. But it could be Duncan, either with Maudie's help or without.* "I'm just being twitchy because I'm impatient. You wait. Master Eschar will come to talk to me soon. He'll find out the truth."

The evening passed, and then the night after it. Jermyn slept badly, his rest troubled by dreams of

Lady Jean's spirit commanding him from the air, and of Brianne in tears. He woke in the morning heavy-headed and exhausted, and still Eschar didn't come. One of the maids brought Jermyn his meals on covered trays, with a separate small dish for Delia. He tried to ask questions, but the maid kept her head down and refused to speak all the while she was with him. When the door opened to let her in, Jermyn could see the guardsman standing at attention in the hall beyond: only one man, but the implication was chilling.

The feeling of being outcast and under suspicion deepened. He had never felt so alone and friendless. By early afternoon, he was convinced he would go insane if something didn't happen. Listlessly, he tossed a wad of paper for Delia to chase. She bounded after it as eagerly as she could, but he could tell that she was acting. So was he.

Why doesn't Master Eschar come? I thought he'd be here—at least to question me. Yes, and to question Delia, too. I wonder if he knows that Lady Jean could talk to anyone's familiar.

Darkly preoccupied, Jermyn didn't look up when the door opened to let in the maid with lunch. "Just put it on the table," he said.

"I will," said a familiar voice. "But I think you'd better pretend to be interested in what we're having for dinner or something. I can't stay long."

"Brianne!" he said, starting up. She was dressed

in one of the maids' uniforms, with her sandy blond hair tied neatly back under a white cap. Her face was set with determination, and her eyes burned. The long night that had left him feeling so helpless and hopeless had obviously stirred her to action. "What are you doing here? If someone sees you—"

She tossed her head impatiently, almost disarranging the cap. "Father and Uncle Eben are closeted in Gran's workroom with that man—Morrenthau—and Master Eschar, of whom, I must say, I thought better. And none of those city guardsmen knows me well enough to recognize me."

"The servants—"

"Where do you think I got the uniform?" she said. "The servants are all on your side. Here, Dee, you'd better have your lunch. Cook made it herself, especially for you."

She set the bowl on the floor, as Jermyn dazedly moved over to the desk. "But your father says I'm guilty," he blurted out, and then he could have kicked himself for mentioning Duncan at all.

"He does," she conceded. "He thinks you're guilty of *something*, anyway, though he doesn't seem too sure of what. But the servants—Phineas, and Cook, and the maids—they watched you after you thought you'd accidentally killed Gran, and they don't think so," she said. "And neither do I, of course."

Her words were a clean, fresh wind blowing

through the room. Jermyn inhaled deeply, then breathed out with an explosive sigh of relief. "That's—that's—thank you. I'm glad you came to visit. If I'd had to sit here much longer, I might have decided I was guilty myself."

"Don't be silly," she said, looking over her shoulder. "Look, I told the guard that I had to clean the water closet. He believed me, but he said I could only have ten minutes. Jermyn, what are we going to do? I thought yesterday that Uncle Eben was going to see the spell Maudie put on us, but then he just went and made everything worse. And so did Master Morrenthau."

"I know," he said helplessly. "Magic like Maudie's is awfully hard to recognize. Have you tried Jemima?"

"This morning," she said, obviously choosing her words cautiously to get them around the Silence. "I went down to the village first thing—I told Father I had a headache and we were out of headache powder. She looked at me sort of funny when I first walked in, but that was all. So I told her you thought I might be a healer, because I thought it might make her look at me really closely, and she did get all excited. She even said she'd set up the formal test for me as soon as she could. But when I tried to tell her how I'd—already been 'tested,' I couldn't."

"I'm not surprised," he said, speaking with equal care. *This isn't so bad*, he realized. *We can almost talk about Mistress Allons's death, if we're careful —better than we could before, anyway. Because now we aren't thinking of telling anyone about it? Maybe. I wish I knew more about the limits of the Silence spell.* "That's close to what Maudie didn't want us to talk about."

"What about Master Eschar?" she asked.

"He couldn't see anything. He isn't a practicing wizard." Jermyn pondered painfully. "I did think, if I could get him alone, I might be able to let him know something was wrong. He's very quick at picking things up. But he won't come near me."

"He hasn't had a chance yet," she said quickly. "Master Morrenthau wanted to do this thing called a Guild spell of long-term sympathetic imaging in the workroom, and he said it had to be done today. Do you know why?"

"I've never even heard of it," he said honestly. "Long-term sympathetic imaging. . . ." He thought a moment. "From the name of the spell, it must have something to do with the impression of herself that your grandmother would have left on her workroom. Maybe Master Morrenthau thinks he can find out how she died by calling up an image of her workroom at the moment of her death."

Brianne frowned. "But isn't that Spirit Calling, like Maudie's Questing? Uncle Eben said that wouldn't work after so much time had passed."

"I don't think it's Spirit Calling," Jermyn said.

"Not exactly, anyway. Maybe it's a special spell of Master Morrenthau's—he's head of the Guild, after all. Or Master Eschar could have researched it for him."

"Well, whatever it is, we can't wait to find out if it works or not," she said. "The important thing is, they'll be busy all afternoon. That gives us an opportunity. We may not get another one soon."

"An opportunity to do what?" he asked guiltily, thinking, *Maybe I can talk her into searching Tower Landing for evidence, including her father's rooms.*

"Someone has to go down to the crypt," she said steadily. "And since we're the only ones who know—you know—about Gran, it's got to be us. If . . . her ghost is wandering, we might be able to find out why." She had to work hard to get some of the words out this time, and it cost her. Perspiration beaded her forehead. "This—Silence thing won't stop us from doing that, will it? I mean, it's just about talking. Isn't it?"

"It is," he said, facing her squarely. He hadn't considered Lady Jean's burial place as a possible source of information. Taking a deep breath, he forced himself to answer her specifically. "That's— a good idea. Revenants do tend to stay close to where their bodies are buried. But do you really want to go down to the crypt?"

She bit her lip, deeply troubled. "No. I just can't think of anything else to do. And we have to do *something*. I'm sorry, Jermyn, but I c-couldn't make myself go down there alone. . . ."

Jermyn went dry-mouthed at the very thought. "Of course you couldn't, and I don't blame you. I couldn't either. Don't even think about it. Only how do I get out of this room to go with you?"

"That's no problem," she said, looking relieved. "When I come back for your tray, I'm to bring the guard his lunch. Your aunt is an herbalist, isn't she?"

"Yes," he said, seeing where she was leading. "You want to slip something into his food?"

"We only need a minute to get past him," she said eagerly. "I thought maybe sleeping powder to make him doze off, but I wasn't sure."

"No, it's too hard to get the dosage right with something like that," he said. "How about stone-root? That will just make him sick to his stomach —and he'll get over it so fast, he'll probably think it was a natural cramp. You ought to have lots of stoneroot in the kitchen, for scouring."

"I'm sure we do," she said. "That's perfect. And you can leave Delia here, so that if he checks the room when he gets back he'll think you're still—"

No, Delia said firmly. *Go, too.*

Jermyn looked at her in surprise; she didn't usually respond when someone else was speaking, even if she understood the words. "Dee wants to come, too, and she has a point. It might help to have her with me, if we need to deal with magic. Does the guard have a key to this room?"

She nodded. "Yes, of course. He let me in. I've got a spare set, though, so I can let you out."

"Then make sure when you leave this time that he knows his key is the *only* key," Jermyn said. "Tell him that Miss Brianne is complaining about not being able to lock and unlock the cellar, or something, because she doesn't have any keys. Can you do that?"

"As easily as Delia can catch a rat," she assured him, then looked troubled. "Jermyn, I never thought—how are we going to get you back in?"

He shrugged. "That's the least of our worries. Maybe you can decoy the guard. If we find something, we'll go straight to Master Eschar anyway."

She nodded again. "Give me half an hour, then. And you better try to eat something, if you can."

He couldn't. The prospect of having something to do made him choke on every bite. Instead, he fastened Delia's pad to his shoulder—so she would have a place to ride in case they had to run—and pressed his ear to the hall door. The wood was thick, but after what seemed like forever he caught a murmur that might have been Brianne's voice. Then, not long after that, he heard the noise of someone running quickly, followed by Brianne's opening the door so suddenly that he almost fell into the hall.

"He's gone," she said unnecessarily. The guard's abandoned dinner tray lay face down on the hall carpet. "Hurry."

"Lock the door," he reminded her.

She did, with shaking hands. "We'll go down the back stairs. I've got one of Phineas's old garden coats for you. Put it on and carry that basket for me. If any guardsman asks, I'll say we're going into the conservatory to repot some flowers."

Jermyn knew it wasn't the prospect of being stopped that was unnerving her; it was their destination. He felt the same way. The trip down the back stairs was uneventful, except for passing one of the maids—who pointedly looked at the floor as they went by.

"That's so she doesn't have to lie if someone asks her whether she's seen us," Brianne whispered, as they entered the chapel. "When she says no, it will be true."

Jermyn nodded tightly. The chapel was empty and dark. Brianne took one of the unlit lanterns from a side niche, lit it, and handed it to him. He took it without comment. It would be dark in the crypt.

He had forgotten the dead-light. Its soft blue glow was waiting for them, though dimmer than it had been the day before. The crypt was illuminated by the dead-light and the lantern from the chapel. Stone carvings cast fantastical shadows along the walls.

On his shoulder, Delia wrinkled her nose in distaste. *Smelly,* she commented fastidiously.

"Do you smell magic?" He extended his own senses slightly. Brianne looked at him, alarmed. He shook his head slightly, to show he was talking to his familiar.

No, Delia answered. *Just old.*

"What is it?" Brianne asked in a hushed voice.

"Delia says it smells old," he told her. "Musty, I guess she means. She can't feel any magic, though, and neither can I."

She swallowed. "There's something—there. By Gran's tomb."

He studied the slab carefully. "I don't see it."

"It's something," she insisted. "Like a haze over the top."

Jermyn took a deep breath. "Well, we'll just have to look closer. Here—hold this."

He handed her the lantern; she took it and hung it on a hook next to the dead-light.

"We'll never be able to lift that stone alone," she told him. "It took three men to get it in place yesterday."

"We don't have to lift it," he said. "Just shift it out of the way."

She nodded tightly. "I suppose if we both push hard, we might be able to wedge it against the wall."

At their first straining effort, the stone scarcely budged. Jermyn braced himself against the corner of the niche for better leverage, and they tried again. And again. On their third groaning try, the slab tilted back, scraping viciously against the rough blocks of the wall. The discordant grating noise made Jermyn's hair stand up, but finally the slab was out of the way.

The shining wood of the coffin lid stared blankly up at them. Jermyn reached down with one hand, then hesitated. "Brianne. . . ."

"You do it," she said, her face taut. Blue shadows from the dead-light made her look uncanny, almost ghostlike. "Please. I—I can't."

Delia clucked sympathetically into Jermyn's ear. He nodded. "All right. If you want."

He took hold of the coffin lid with both hands, half expecting it to be nailed shut, but it came up with a single smooth motion. Lady Jean Allons, her face shrouded in white net, lay peacefully in front of them.

Brianne gasped and started back against Jermyn. He could feel her shaking.

"It's all right, Brianne," he said gently. "There's no reason to be afraid."

She pulled away and reached down with one trembling hand. She didn't—quite—touch the body.

"No," she said, her voice ragged and soft. "No, there isn't. But—oh, Jermyn, can't you see? She wasn't like this yesterday. Look at her. Just look!"

He tried, focusing mind and magic on the open coffin. For a long moment, there was nothing. Then, as Delia stirred uneasily, he sensed rather than saw a soft vapor rising from the body—like the shimmering mist in Maudie's hut. Delicate silver tendrils lifted toward the dark ceiling of the crypt, like white lace glowing in the moonlight. Tensing, he stepped away, pulling Brianne with him.

"I see something," he admitted. "But I don't know what, and I don't know what we can do about it, either. I think we'd better get out of here."

"In a minute," she whispered. Then, more loudly, she said, "Gran? Gramma, are you there?"

Something was. The lace tendrils spread out into an oddly familiar pattern. Jermyn blinked. *Where have I seen that before?* The web meant that Lady Jean's ghost wasn't *there*, but she was connected to this place. To her body, as most revenants were. Only where was *she*?

From his shoulder, Delia hissed. *Bad magic.*

"What is it?" Jermyn said, stepping up beside Brianne. In the back of his mind, a little voice yammered that he must be insane to stay here, that he should be grabbing Brianne and running for daylight, but he couldn't help himself. "No one's working magic down here, Dee. What do you smell?"

Up! she said, her claws digging into the pad. *Up up up!*

"The workroom!" Brianne cried, echoing Delia's

urgency. "We're right below it here. Whatever the trouble is, it's in Gran's workroom."

The web glowed more sullenly against the darkness of the crypt, its lines of force twisting wildly upward—pulled by something that Jermyn couldn't see. He felt his own gut twist in a sympathetic agony.

"Something's wrong, all right," he said, following the line of magic upward through the tower. "She must be *haunting* the workroom. And Master Morrenthau won't be expecting a ghost, especially not so strong a one. When he casts his spell, the overflow of psychic energy will kill him and maybe everyone else in the room, too. Come on—we've got to stop him!"

Jermyn plunged for the stairs, with Brianne right behind him. They pounded through the chapel and up the back stairs to the central hall. When they passed the guard back on duty in front of Jermyn's door, he shouted at them to stop. Jermyn dropped Delia at his feet; she wove a quick twisting path between the guardsman's legs, and he went down with a shout.

The workroom door was locked. Jermyn could see, spread out evenly around the edges of the frame, the faint glow that meant magic.

"We're too late," he said, panting slightly. "They've started."

The glow deepened from yellow to cherry red

as he watched. Then it started to burn a brilliant blue-white.

"When will it happen?" Brianne asked. "The backlash, I mean."

"As soon as Master Morrenthau starts to release the spell," Jermyn said. "He'll lose control of it then."

"Well, we can't just stand here." She glanced quickly down the corridor: more guardsmen. "Uh-oh. There's the Commander of the Guard—Baker, his name is. He isn't going to like this. Can you get in?"

"I don't think so," he said, touching the door with one finger and then yanking it back from the heat. "Your grandmother's protections are engaged. They ought to have died when she did—at least the personal ones—but something about her ghost haunting the Tower must be reactivating them."

Je'm'n do, Delia commanded him sternly from his feet. *Not talk.*

"Yes, all right," he said. "We'll get in there somehow."

The guard Commander was a burly man with a thick black mustache; he strode up the hallway as if it were a battlefield. "What's going on?" he said furiously. "You people shouldn't be here."

Brianne whirled. "Commander Baker, we've got to open this door right now!" she said commandingly, every inch Lady Jean's granddaughter. "Journeyman Graves says that something is going seriously wrong with the magic in the workroom. My father and my uncle are in that room. We *must* take immediate action."

"There's black art involved," Jermyn put in. He waved at Delia. "My familiar senses it."

Baker pulled up short and glanced worriedly at the door. The arcane light was stronger now, so that even someone without magical sensitivity could see it. The Commander might not be a wizard, but he didn't look like a fool, and only a fool didn't fear magic gone wrong. "Journeyman Graves is confined to quarters," he said stiffly. "I have my orders."

"And I have my oath to the Guild," Jermyn said impatiently. "You can arrest me later. For now, I'm the only wizard you've got, and we must get into that room."

"I don't know," the Commander said slowly. He looked from the burning door to Jermyn and back again, frowning.

At least he's willing to listen, Jermyn thought. *That's something.*

Clustered around Baker, his men looked nervous and confused. "What do you propose to do?" the Commander asked.

"Can you break the door down, Jermyn?" Brianne asked.

He hesitated. "It's too strong for a direct assault.

If I could find even a crack or a hole, that might—Delia."

Yes, Je'm'n? she said, putting her forepaws on his foot and looking up.

He squatted beside her, thinking the words and speaking them out loud at the same time, so everyone could hear. "Can you find me a hole in the wall that leads into the workroom? A rat hole, maybe?"

Yes, Je'm'n! she said, and put her nose to the ground.

"A rat hole?" one of the guardsman said. "What good will that do?"

"Mistress Allons wouldn't have blocked something like that specifically," Jermyn said, trying to keep the irritation out of his voice. "I might be able to work with it. Brianne, can you get us into all the rooms on this floor?"

She hauled her keys out of her apron. "Watch me. Commander? Are you with us or against us?"

Baker was examining the door. Pulling on a pair of heavy leather gauntlets, he tried the latch. It didn't budge. The leather sizzled as he jerked his hands away.

He nodded decisively. "That does it. I'm no wizard, but I've worked with Master Morrenthau often enough. He would have warned me if he were going to seal the room, or if he were going to make the door burn like that. We'd better get in there and see what's up. Stemmin, Vance, evacuate the household staff. Peters and Wolmark, with me. The rest of you, fan out around the Tower and guard it. I'm not sure exactly what we're up against, so be alert for anything," he finished grimly. "Journeyman Graves?"

"It's up to my familiar," Jermyn said aloud, all the while thinking, *Commander Baker is not only willing to listen, he's willing to trust me. He didn't even seem too angry that I was out of my rooms. Why?* "Delia? Which way do we go?"

Delia found a hole in the second room they tried, in the linen closet. Recklessly, Jermyn threw sheets and towels over his shoulder, burrowing through the piles of neatly ironed and folded cloth until he reached it. *A rat hole, all right*, he thought, running his fingers around the edges. *Good girl, Dee.* It didn't lead directly into the workroom but rather into a narrow space behind the molding. Jermyn closed his eyes and extended his senses, blessing Delia's keen nose; the scent must have been far from fresh. No rats had lived in this hole for rodent generations.

"Yes, that's it," he said softly. "This will do."

He knelt on the floor, one hand hovering over the rat hole and the other on Delia's back. Power flowed along his fingertips in an ever-increasing stream. He willed it to spread, to push open—like a bellows inflating, like a river flooding over its banks. The hole in the wall screamed in protest, then widened.

"Get back!" Jermyn shouted.

A waterfall of wood and masonry cascaded on either side of the linen closet, reducing half of the room into a pile of rubble, but it was the magic barrier—Lady Jean's protections—that kept them out, not the physical wall. Jermyn could see the arc of protective sorcery clearly now, shining through the debris. It rippled, like water, and he saw that he'd weakened it. *Not enough, though. Needs more pressure—there, where the waves curve. I think I can do it. Dee?*

Delia grunted her acknowledgment as he reached for more power—and the rubble fragmented into shards. He coughed, batting at clouds of dust as he tried to see through the newly created hole in the wall. Brianne grabbed his shoulder as he lunged forward with Delia at his heels, and together they stumbled into the workroom. The magic flowed around them, opening to let them in and then closing the way behind them again—resealing the path against anyone who didn't have the sorcery to break through the weakened defenses. Baker and his men didn't make it; Jermyn heard the Commander shouting angrily behind them, but it was too late to explain or apologize.

He and Brianne—and Delia—were in, but they were on their own.

13

BLACK ARTIST

IT SEEMED almost anticlimactic. The room was so quiet that if it hadn't been for the crackle of sorcery in the air, he wouldn't have known that anything was going on at all. At his feet, Delia bristled. *Bad*, she said. *Bad magic*.

Eben Allons and Master Eschar stood facing each other on either side of a squared circle, each outside the circle but inside the corners of the square. Spellcaster Morrenthau knelt at the center, his arms crossed over his chest. His eyes were dazed, and he didn't look up. Shards of a broken spell trailed from his fingertips and over his head, forming an obscene halo. *That's a trap spell,* Jermyn realized, recognizing the fragments. *A powerful one. So that's what they were doing.*

Duncan was slumped to the floor outside the circle, behind Morrenthau. Magic pinned him down, and his eyes were closed.

"Father!" Brianne cried, and started to go to him; Jermyn held her back.

"Don't," he told her sympathetically. Of course Duncan was the guilty one. *Maybe I should have tried to tell her, after all.* "He's caught in what's left of a trap spell. He must have triggered it somehow. If you touch him, you'll be caught in it with him."

"But he isn't a sorcerer," she said, anguished. "He *can't* be a black artist."

"He isn't," Eben Allons said, glaring at Jermyn with sheer rage. "I am. But they would have thought he was if you hadn't interfered." He moved his hands in an intricate pattern.

Delia hissed. *Bad man!*

The black magician is Eben? Jermyn thought incredulously, stunned by the very idea. *But it's Duncan in the trap spell. I like Eben!*

New ideas tumbled through his mind, sorting themselves into order. *So Eben is the black artist,* he thought, struggling with it. *He must have fought with his mother so he'd have an excuse to stay away from her. He was going to be a wizard before he entered the Church. As a priest, he works with the*

235

Powers all the time. That would cover up most magical activities. But why did he kill his mother? Unless . . . He would feel stupid if he weren't so scared.

"Jermyn, duck!" Eschar shouted, throwing himself into the middle of Eben's half-formed spell. Eben pulled at something—Jermyn couldn't see what or how, but it made his insides twist. Frantically, he lurched against Brianne, pulling her down to the floor with him.

Eschar stood half-crouching, magically frozen in the middle of his spring. The interrupted spell reformed around him, and his jaw strained with the effort of speaking. "Give it up, Eben," he whispered, struggling to get the words out. "Too late. Morrenthau and I both know. . . ."

"Give it up? Not likely," Eben said, sneering. He pushed at the comatose Duncan with one foot. "Your little sympathetic-imaging spell only flushed Duncan—I was prepared for this experiment. If the children hadn't interrupted us, I would have had no difficulty in convincing you that my brother-in-law was the villain."

"We were down in the crypt," Jermyn said unevenly, climbing to his feet and thinking furiously, trying to buy time. He motioned Brianne to stay on the floor, but she rolled over and got to her knees beside him. Not looking down, he thought quickly at Delia, who started edging her way around the circle. *All right, it's Eben who's guilty. Deal with it.*

"We felt something strange, and decided we ought to come see what it was."

"So that was it," Eben said, grimacing in annoyance. "I'd forgotten that the crypt is in a direct line with this room. A pity you're so sensitive—ah, well. At least you had intelligence enough to make your entrance with no one but Brianne for witness. I take it you convinced the guards to let you deal with possible sorcery on your own?" He smiled slightly at the guarded shock on Jermyn's face. "Fair enough. What made you suspect me?"

"Nothing," Jermyn said. "I knew someone had used the backlash from my shield spell to kill Lady Jean, but I thought it was Duncan." Absently, he noticed that Maudie's Silence had vanished, swept away in the rush of sorcery. *That's luck. Or maybe not luck, exactly.*

Eben snorted. "Duncan? So you're not so smart after all. You're just a foolish little Guild magic-maker, like Eschar and Morrenthau. Even if Duncan had studied the black art, sorcery at that level would have fried him if he'd tried to work with it. I, on the other hand, am a priest—and as good a wizard as any in the Guild. I know all about power. You might even have seen my touch in the breaking of the crystal, if you hadn't been too young and too untried—and too stupid to see anything."

"I figured out that the person who broke the crystal was the one who killed Mistress Allons,"

Jermyn said steadily, over Brianne's horrified gasp. Master Eschar was frozen still, but his face was taut with encouragement. *Yes*, he mouthed. *Go!* Jermyn tried not to let the sudden leap of gratification in his heart distract him. "That was aimed at me, wasn't it? You were trying to get rid of me then."

"With you either dead or drained of power, things would have gone back to the way they were before," Eben said, shrugging. "Pity it didn't work."

"The thing that's confused me all along is the motive," Jermyn went on, trying to sound conversational. "Brianne inherits the greatest part of the estate, with her father as guardian. I thought *he* was going to contest the will so he could keep Brianne away from Guild training, but now I think that was really your idea. You wouldn't have wanted Brianne trained in the Guild, or by anyone but you. It would have been too dangerous for you."

"I *did* want to teach little Brianne myself," Eben told him. "Perceptive of you to realize that."

"Thank you," Jermyn said politely. Beside him, Brianne trembled slightly. He slipped one hand beneath her elbow and pressed reassuringly. "But Mistress Allons wasn't killed because of the estate. She was killed because she got in the way of your attempt to trap me, and you were afraid that she'd find out about you. She took her responsibilities and her oath to the Wizards' Guild seriously. If she had discovered that her son was practicing black magic, she would have accused him formally."

For a moment, he thought Eben was going to argue. Then the man relaxed, laughing slightly. "So I was right. It was all over when you came breaking through that wall and disrupted my focus. For a journeyman, you do have flair. No need to be so dramatic—the door would have done as well."

"It wouldn't open," Jermyn said. "Lady Jean's personal protections activated when Morrenthau cast the spell."

"Eh? They couldn't have," Eben said, frowning. His right hand moved slightly, sorcery spilling from it in long, fetid streams. "Mother's personal protections died when she did. It's all your fault, you know. I'd been working my little experiments for years without her noticing. If you hadn't come and started her doing magic again, she might have died in happy ignorance."

"What were you planning to do then?" Jermyn asked, genuinely curious.

Eben shrugged. "Oh, then my dear niece would have entered my household—I doubt her father would have lived much longer. In fact, I'm sure he wouldn't have. Yes, Brianne, I had plans for you. I could have made you a spellmaker, as I almost did with my sister, your mother, before you. Everyone is so emphatic that a spellmaker must not be political. I've always thought it would be interesting to see what one could accomplish politically, if properly instructed. Then, when I finally received the promotion to a city parish, which Mother kept preventing, you would have come with me. After that, who knows? With my—knowledge and skills, and your talent, the whole world might have been ours for the asking."

Brianne's voice was thick with horror. "You would have used me," she said. "You'd have made me—made me—" She couldn't finish the thought.

"The Church wasn't enough for you, was it," Jermyn said, disgusted. "*Or* the Guild. You wanted everything."

"Power is power, my boy," Eben said. "The mindless prejudice that the Guild has against certain forms of it has always irritated me."

"I see," Jermyn said. "How many people in Land's End were in on your experiments? Black artists always have to have a circle of lesser minds or talents to dominate. Was Maudie one of yours?"

"Don't be ridiculous," Eben snapped. "She's just an ignorant old woman, far too weak a talent to be worth bothering with."

"She figured out what you were up to, though, didn't she?" Jermyn said, guessing shrewdly. "I bet she was a danger to you, even if she wouldn't go to the authorities herself."

"No one was a danger to me," Eben said coldly. "Not even my mother. Certainly no pathetic, uneducated country granny could ever pose any kind of a threat."

Delia was half-way around the circle now, still creeping slowly. Once shielded by Duncan's fallen body, she started to move faster.

"Well, you sure didn't seem to like Maudie much," Jermyn said, trying to seem casual. "What about Jemima? I thought she was awfully strong for a journeyman healer. Did you use her?"

"You disappoint me," Eben said, his satisfaction restored. "Corrupting a healer is difficult—I took good care to guard myself against Jemima. Later, perhaps, when Brianne is older, I may have a use for healers. Not yet."

"It wouldn't have worked, you know," Jermyn told him. "Brianne isn't a spellmaker. Mistress Allons could have told you that."

Eben snorted. "Mother was blinded by Duncan's prejudice, and by the untimely death of my sister. Brianne is certainly a spellmaker. She reeks of earth magic."

"She's a healer, like Jemima," Jermyn told him, taking a certain amount of pleasure in contradicting him at last. "Healers are earth wizards, after a fashion. But they aren't spellmakers."

The man's eyes narrowed. "Nonsense. My plans are at worst only delayed, not prevented."

"They are, too, prevented," Brianne said. Her voice shook, but held steady. "Because I'm not going to cooperate. And you can't trick me any more."

Good girl, Jermyn thought to himself, wishing he dared look at her. *Help me out. We're nearly there.* Delia was almost in position. He wiped his free palm on his tunic. "You can't hide anymore, either," he said aloud. "Why don't you listen to Master Eschar and give up?"

"Oh, really," Eben said, waving one hand dismissively. "Master Morrenthau—and, I am afraid, even you, young Jermyn—will scarcely survive the breaking of this spell. It is always dangerous to interrupt a magician at work, after all. As for Master Eschar and Duncan, a judicious pruning and rearranging of their memories will serve. It's a complex spell, but, as I said, I have come prepared."

"What about *my* memory?" Brianne asked, lifting her chin. "Or have you decided to kill me, too?"

"Why, no," he said, sounding amused. "I haven't waited for you this long only to lose you at the finish. I am afraid, though, that the shocks of the last few days have been too much for you, poor little girl. When you've recovered from your breakdown—and I promise that you will be given the best of care—I'm certain you'll see things my way."

"I doubt it," she said coldly.

"I doubt you can rearrange Master Eschar's memory so easily either," Jermyn said, looking at his apprentice-master. The Theoretician managed a slight nod of acknowledgement. "He's no fool. He came into this room prepared to trap you, after all."

"What do you mean?" Eben asked, sounding unsure of himself for the first time. "The spell of long-term sympathetic imaging was merely to re-create the moment in which Mother died. All I had to do was arrange matters so that her spirit-image would seem to implicate Duncan."

Jermyn snorted. "And you thought that would be enough? If the spell hadn't gone wrong, you'd already have learned better. I'm sure of it. Brianne, do you remember I told you before we went into the crypt that I'd never heard of a Guild spell of long-term sympathetic imaging?" She nodded. "That's because Master Eschar made it up."

"That isn't true," Eben said sharply. "I'd never heard of the spell before, but—Eschar and Morren-thau suspected Duncan. They even suspected him of corrupting *you*, Eschar told me."

"You don't know him very well if you really believe that," Jermyn said scornfully. "He wouldn't tell anyone whom he suspected until he had some proof. That's a broken trap spell that's holding Dun-can, not a 'spell of imaging.' Master Morrenthau must have set it to catch whoever tried to interfere with what he was doing, since the only person who might be interested in hiding the truth is the mur-derer. You just shifted it onto Duncan for a moment, but that wouldn't have lasted long."

"They *can't* have suspected," Eben said, his jaw working. He looked from Morrenthau to the immobile Theoretician with hatred. "My familiar spirit is a powerful air demon. It would have told me if I were in danger."

"Did it tell you when Brianne and I were about to break through the wall?" Jermyn asked. "That's the trouble with air spirits. They don't really like the people who create them and order them around. This creating-demons stuff is kind of useless."

"You don't know what you're talking about," Eben said. "Why, with my spirit, I can fly."

"You *think* you can fly," Jermyn corrected condescendingly. "The drugs black artists take enhance magical abilities, but they also cause hallucinations. It's easy for a spirit to make you think he's carrying you over the kingdoms of earth and air when you're all doped up. Master Eschar explained it to me once. It all sounds pretty silly."

"Silly?" Eben took a step forward, almost into the square. "I'll show you silly, you—boy!"

Eben lifted his hands, the spell that Master Eschar had interrupted again glittering darkly between them. But this time, Jermyn was ready. Holding the structure of the shield spell firmly in mind, he flipped it into place. Magic caught magic in a coruscating burst of light.

Eben chuckled unpleasantly. "That won't save you," he said. "I solved that spell the first time you used it, in the conservatory. It was such a splendidly overdone piece of work, with so much more energy than you needed floating all through it. I knew you'd use it if I rigged the scaffold to fall, and you didn't disappoint me. My plan worked perfectly then, and now all I have to do is—this!"

He held his two hands out in front of him, palms facing each other about a foot apart. A dark shape started to swirl between them, a shape with arms and red eyes—Eben's familiar spirit.

Jermyn gulped and forced himself not to look away.

"We'll start with the master, I believe," Eben purred. "Rank should offer *some* benefits. William, I believe that the boy is right about you—it wouldn't be safe to let you live. Whether or not you suspected me, you always did have an annoying habit of finding things out. . . ."

The spirit reached its long, impossibly thin arms across the circle. Eschar shuddered as they touched him. Brianne screamed.

"Now, Dee!" Jermyn cried, reversing the normal flow of magic along the familiar-link—sending power *to* his familiar instead of pulling it through her for his own use. "Get him!"

From behind Eben, the furry black-and-white shape dashed across the circle, her tail smearing the marks. The power she contained—more than any familiar usually held—protected her and got her through the barrier. Savagely, she bit the renegade priest in the ankle, her whole body quivering with rage.

Once she was in the circle, so was Jermyn—he gathered his energy and ripped at the already broken spell, unraveling it still further.

Eben yelled. His familiar spirit drifted away as his concentration wavered, out of reach. "You— you—"

Ropes, Jermyn thought feverishly. *Make ropes of magic holding him—chains of sorcery. He's got to be about out of strength, his reserves exhausted. If I can only hold him long enough for Master Morrenthau to recover—*

But the broken pieces of the original trap spell got in his way; he could feel them pulling at him as he tried to set up his own spell, forcing his magic aside. Eben staggered, but then regained his balance.

"Not bad, for a mere journeyman," he said, breathing heavily. "But *I* am master of an art you never dreamed of. . . ."

A thick flood of power caught at Jermyn's soul, pulling at him. He fought for breath, for light. The familiar-link to Delia glowed dimly against the oily darkness. Desperately he caught at it.

Je'm'n! her mind-voice cried at him. *Je'm'n, the lady!*

Lady? What lady? Oh. Oh, yes. His mind cleared at Delia's touch, reducing the world to patterns of energy and light. He almost nodded in recognition, amazed at his own sudden calm. *I thought that web looked familiar. It isn't the workroom that's haunted—it's the crystal.* He reached out through every pathway that was open to him, seeking for one that he had thought long closed. *There—that's it. The line into the broken crystal. You've always been able to think your way into just about any crystal. You could activate your aunt's when you were seven years old. All you need to do is touch— open the way through journeyman-master link— open for the vengeful spirit seeking justice.*

Eben screamed, a terrible gibbering sound. He lurched backward against the table. Taking shape in front of him was the spirit-form of Lady Jean, tall, elegant, and uncanny. She looked down at her son with contempt in her eyes.

"It was the crystal, of course," Jermyn said, speaking very clearly. "You wouldn't be afraid of an ordinary revenant, not with the sort of magical protections you've probably got, but you forgot about the crystal. She must have been working with it, trying to see what went wrong, when you directed that backlash at her. She'd have understood then what was going on—what you were. That's why she knew she had to fight to stay. When your spell hit, she was able to fasten herself into the broken web. She couldn't save herself, but she could try to warn the rest of us. And maybe even do more, with a little help from some friends." *From Delia and me, offering a channel for power into this room, into Eben's own soul. . . .*

"No," Eben said, holding up his arms in front of his face in a futile gesture. "Mother, no! Don't!"

Lady Jean's voice rolled through Jermyn's mind like the sound of rushing water. *False, Eben Allons*, it said. *False son, false brother, false wizard, false priest. Bear the burden of that falseness—take back your broken oaths.*

Power poured through the room like sunlight. Jermyn fell to his knees, shielding his eyes. Somehow he found Delia in his lap and bent over her, sheltering her and himself against the storm. *Good Deedee*, he told her, immensely proud of her. *Good girl. Hang on.* She nuzzled him affectionately.

Eben screamed again, a keening, an eerie sound that went on and on and on until all the world seemed swallowed up in it. Then it faded.

Jermyn opened his eyes. Master Eschar was picking himself up from the hearth, offering a hand to Morrenthau, who seemed disoriented but otherwise unhurt. Brianne bent over her father, wiping fresh tears from her eyes as he stirred.

Eben had collapsed face down on the floor; Jermyn couldn't tell if he was breathing or not. There was no sign of anyone else.

It was over.

14

THE PARTING GIFT

THE NEXT several days were confusing. It helped that Felix Morrenthau had brought his own crystal from the city, so messages could fly back and forth to the Guild. Eben's accomplices—Master Eschar said that *victims* might be a better word—had to be discovered. The broken wall would have to be repaired and the workroom cleaned. Lawyer Oldcastle, as the local justice, had to be convinced of both the crime and its solution.

Duncan Campbell required healing, but Jemima said immediately that he would recover in a day or two.

She came out of his room after only a few minutes of examination. "He'll be fine," she reported to Master Eschar and Master Morrenthau. Jermyn noticed a faint half flush staining her cheeks; she seemed embarrassed. He wondered why. "Brianne is going to sit with him for a while. Whatever Eben did to him, the trap spell didn't hurt him. He just needs to rest."

"Splendid," Eschar said.

Morrenthau frowned. He was annoyed that his trap spell had gone so thoroughly awry. "We'll have to take Duncan back to the city with us, for further investigation. And Brianne, too, of course."

"Surely you don't believe that Duncan is guilty of black magic," Jemima said, outraged.

"Brianne!" Jermyn said at the same time, hotly. "No one can think she's part of all this."

"We'll have to investigate—" Master Morrenthau started.

Eschar interrupted him, unsuccessfully trying to hide a smile. "Calm down, both of you. Jemima, I assure you that no one who was present at that horrendous scene in the workroom could think that Duncan was anything but a dupe. But we will have to track down the other members of the conspiracy, and Duncan's knowledge of the district could prove invaluable in that. So could yours, for that matter. Perhaps you might consider returning with us?"

"Well, I don't know," she said. For some reason,

she was now blushing furiously. "It depends on Duncan."

"And as for Brianne, it is even more obvious that she is innocent," Eschar went on, glancing at Jermyn. "She may have insights of her own to add to her father's, of course, but the real reason she should come with us is that it's about time she started her schooling. Jemima says that she's going to be a very powerful healer one day, and she'll need to study with a master. All right, Jermyn?"

"All right," he said slowly. "But what will her father say? He's been pretty much against her working any kind of sorcery all along. Will he approve of her being a healer?"

"He has little choice, now," Jemima said, looking satisfied. Her pleasure in Brianne's gift was almost funny. "True healers are rare enough that no one with sufficient talent and desire need ever fear lacking the training. Duncan will just have to adjust."

"I expect he will," Eschar said smoothly. "The man has been a fool for quite long enough, it seems to me. . . ."

Jemima blushed again, even more furiously. Jermyn studied her with new interest. *Jemima and Duncan? I suppose it's possible. She's a healer and Brianne said he counts healing as magic, so maybe that's kept them apart.*

Morrenthau wasn't interested in blushes, or

romance. He cleared his throat meaningfully. "It's going to take most of the winter to track down every member of the black art circle. What about this hedgewitch, for example? Old Maudie?"

"Gone to ground," Eschar said. "Baker and his men tore her hut apart and couldn't find a trace of her. Jemima, your opinion?"

"Maudie's lived around these parts since long before I was born," the healer said. She glanced briefly at Jermyn, and he nodded. Between them, they had decided that Brianne's lessons with the hedgewitch were none of Master Morrenthau's business. Brianne was a healer now, and the Healers' Guild would take care of her. "I've kept an eye on her, according to my Guild's practice as well as yours, but she's never done any harm."

"I think she was afraid of Eben," Jermyn said quietly. He'd told Morrenthau about Maudie's Questing and the Silence, but not in any detail. "Maybe she was even trying to help us, as best she could. Eben said that she wasn't a member of his circle."

"Hmm, so he did," Morrenthau said, pursing his lips. "Well, I should question her anyway. Baker and his men should be able to find her eventually."

Jermyn didn't comment, but he went looking for Maudie himself early the next morning. Before he left, he asked Cook for a tin of sugar from the pantry. She looked at him curiously but gave him what he asked for with no questions. Then he put Delia on his shoulder and slipped out the cloister entrance when no one was watching.

The sugar was a *thank you* and *farewell*—it was all he could think to offer.

When he reached the hut, he was surprised to see Towser tied to the door. The old dog was half-asleep in a patch of winter sun and didn't seem to notice Delia on Jermyn's shoulder.

Delia stirred slightly.

Behave, Jermyn told her sternly. *He's tied and can't go after you.*

Huh, she answered. *Silly dog.*

Towser whined at Jermyn, wagging his tail dubiously, but he didn't try to stop them from going into the hut.

Inside, there was a banked fire on the hearth, but no Maudie.

Jermyn had no doubt that she was nearby, listening. "Thank you, Mistress," he said aloud, setting the sugar on the table. "I'd stay close to the earth for a little while, if I were you. Master Morrenthau is a smart man—it won't take him very long to figure out that he might as well leave you alone."

No answer—not a flicker of response—but he knew that she'd heard him somehow.

When we get back to the city, I'll talk to Master Eschar about hedgewitchery and earth magic, he thought, pulling his cloak tighter as he turned to leave. *He'll be interested. If I tell him now, he might feel that he has to do something official about Maudie.*

When Captain Baker and his men found Maudie's hut, it was empty and cold. Master Morrenthau was irritated, but eventually he decided that it would be a waste of time to mount a full-scale search for one elderly hedgewitch. He had found Eben's notes by that time, and several other promising clues.

"I doubt that this Maudie knows much, in any case," Jermyn heard him tell Master Eschar. "She'll probably surface when all the fuss is over. Right now, I'm more concerned about the actual members of the circle. We need to find out who they are *and* how they managed to stay undetected for so long. This sort of thing should be dealt with firmly. I'm thinking of ordering a formal investigating team to come north even before the spring thaw."

"A good thought," Eschar said. "There's no need to decide anything in haste, however. We should know where we stand in a few more days."

There were no decisions to be made about the fate of Eben Allons. He remained in the entranced state he had entered the moment he'd seen his mother's spirit hovering in the air in front of him. Jermyn saw him once, as he was being carried out of the workroom under guard.

"*Catatonia mysticae*, and probably just as well," Master Eschar remarked later. He and Jermyn were in the library, reviewing the catalog of the books which they had jointly inherited. There were a great many of them. It was Jermyn's considered opinion that Master Eschar was going to need a larger library. No, a larger *house*. "The Guild wants his hide for what he did, and the penalties due a forsworn priest are even worse. As it is, he'll spend the rest of his days in an asylum somewhere, under armed guard. A mercy, really."

Jermyn wasn't so sure. Eben's empty eyes haunted him.

"What's *catatonia mysticae*?" he asked.

"A magically induced condition resembling certain forms of extreme insanity," the Theoretician said didactically, as he leaned forward to jot a note to himself on the list of books he was holding. "Whether or not the personality is indeed destroyed is still under debate. In fact, certain scholars hypothesize that the mind simply withdraws itself absolutely and permanently from external stimuli—"

"Master Eschar," Jermyn said reprovingly.

Eschar stopped, then smiled. "Sorry. I *was* getting carried away. I take it you want to know if Eben is going to recover. He isn't."

"I think I understood that much," Jermyn said. "What I really want to know is what caused him to—to go inside himself like that in the first place."

"I don't think I can answer that one," Eschar told him, sighing. "Jean had a very forceful personality, and Eben would have been under an almost intolerable strain these past few months. Between that trap spell that Felix threw at him and your own actions, he must have been half-mad already. Then, to see his mother, whom he'd killed—to feel her presence. . . ."

He fell silent. No one really liked talking about that part of it: that by murdering his mother, Eben had somehow caused her to be held between life and death. Perhaps by her own choice, perhaps just in confusion. Master Morrenthau, at least, thought that Lady Jean had died so suddenly and so unnaturally that she'd been unaware of what had happened, and that that was what had caused her spirit to linger.

Jermyn saw no point in arguing, but he wasn't convinced.

"At least Mistress Allons is at rest now," he said.

Eschar nodded. The priest who had been brought in from a neighboring province had assured them of that. He'd reconsecrated both the chapel and the crypt and said that he sensed no trace of a vengeful or grieving spirit imprisoned anywhere in the tower.

When the theoretician didn't speak, Jermyn went on, "So you and Spellcaster Morrenthau did plan the whole thing. Didn't you?"

"We did," Eschar said, obviously as relieved as Jermyn to shift the conversation. "We discussed possible contingency tactics on the journey up, in fact. I was sorry to have to pretend to suspect you, but we needed something that would distract both Duncan and Eben."

"Oh, I never believed for a minute that you really thought I was guilty," Jermyn said, as airily as he could. It didn't entirely succeed; Eschar's eyes were twinkling at him. "Delia was a little upset with you, though. And you don't want to hear what she wanted to do to Master Morrenthau."

"I expect I don't," Eschar said cheerfully. "At least not until we're safely back in the city and I needn't feel responsible for you anymore."

They worked awhile without speaking. Then Jermyn brought up something else.

"Do you think Eben had anything to do with Brianne's mother's death?" he asked quietly.

Eschar ran one hand through his hair, as he did when a problem disturbed him. "We'll never know the whole story. She's dead, and he isn't going to be answering any questions. Better to let it remain an accident, I would say. I suspect, though, that the answer is yes. If he assumed that she had spellmaker capabilities, as he certainly did assume about Brianne, then he may have tried to use her."

As he planned to use Brianne, Jermyn thought, the idea making his mouth taste sour. "Would he have been able to do that?"

"Not for long, if at all," Eschar said positively. "He was a fool to think that he could. No one *uses* an earth wizard, whether healer or spellmaker. There is something about earth magic that prevents such personal manipulation. Of course, he might have persuaded her to assist him independently in some way . . . I don't know. In any case, Brianne is safe now, thanks be to all the Powers."

Jermyn silently echoed the thanksgiving.

Eventually, Felix Morrenthau elected to stay in Land's End, to begin the investigation in the province. About half the troop of guardsmen would be staying with him. The rest, including Commander Baker and the prisoner, were due to leave for the city well ahead of him; Master Eschar's party would travel with them. The Weather Hall promised a cold, fair winter, with no snow in the immediate forecast. They would still have to travel slowly because of the weight of so many passengers, but the journey should be reasonably uneventful. In order to help keep the weight lower, the Theoretician had limited himself to three boxes of books that he absolutely *had* to bring back with him.

There was only one thing left for Jermyn to do. A few days before they were scheduled to depart, he climbed the stairs to the workroom with Delia at his heels. He touched the door, and it swung open—no more magical protections, no more locks. All the sensitive and delicate material had been removed.

He spared a glance for the immense hole in the inner wall. Someone had tacked a sheet over the empty space, but that only made the damage look more impressive.

Big magic, Delia commented proudly.

"Yes, it was," he said, looking around the room for the broken crystal. No one had bothered with it since the disaster. There simply hadn't been time.

Carefully, Jermyn spread the velvet cloth out on the table and placed the large section of broken crystal in the center of it. Then he picked up the broken-off fragment in his right hand, holding it by the outer, faceted side so that he didn't cut himself on the sharp edges.

"Sit there, Dee, will you?" he said, pointing at the other side of the table. She curled her forepaws under herself and watched him intently. "This shouldn't take long."

He placed his left hand around the side of the

base of the crystal and held the broken chunk, sharp side down, over the place where it ought to be, slowly bringing it into position without quite allowing either piece to touch. As he did, he remembered Kate's *On the Art of Spellmaking*, the book he'd had so much trouble understanding.

More than most magical persuasions, spellmaking is an art, he'd read the first time without comprehension. *The practice of this art, as of all arts, requires skill, knowledge, and understanding, as well as observation and experiment—the tools of science. These things assist the spellmaker in the practice of his profession as comprehension of the laws of perspective and studies in anatomy benefit the painter. However, the core of spellmaking, the soul of it, is the creative imagination: an insistence that whatever the human mind imagines to be true may be perceived as such, and so made real.*

Jermyn half smiled: it sounded so complicated, the way Kates had said it. *Well, it is complicated*, he thought. *So simple that it's complicated, like Mistress Allons's privacy spell. But I know what it means now.* Ultimately, he'd realized, all a spellmaker had to do was *imagine* the spell—correctly, carefully, and with balance and control. He did so now, concentrating on mentally drawing crystal lattices in air between the two broken pieces; imagining the magical force pulling them together, fitting them into place as neatly as two pieces of a puzzle. He had to imagine the web of magic in the crystal spell, too. It was tricky, a narrowly useful piece of magic that neither he nor anyone else would ever be likely to need again, since it was usually easier to create a new crystal than to repair an old one. But his imaging worked. The two pieces of crystal heated briefly between his palms, glowing a soft silver. When he took his hands away, they were one.

Good Je'm'n, Delia observed. *Good magic.*

"It is," he said, but he didn't take his eyes away from the crystal. One thing left. . . . The glow didn't fade. Instead, it built softly, becoming so bright that he had to blink or look away. He blinked, and suddenly she was there.

Jean Allons.

Well done, Jermyn, she said softly, her spirit presence as gently welcoming as it had been urgent before. *My last journeyman. You have the way of it now.*

"Then I am a spellmaker?" he asked aloud. She wasn't in the room with him—she was more of a vision in the mind's eye, but he didn't doubt her presence.

You were always a spellmaker, she said. *You simply needed to learn what that meant. The crystal is truly yours now, as I said it would be in my will. I would be pleased if you would offer it to your successor, when that time comes.*

If he hadn't believed that she'd stayed of her own

free will, her spirit remaining in the crystal, he knew the absolute truth of it now. She was calmly accepting, even matter-of-fact, about her own presence.

"I'll do that," he promised her. "Of course I will."

"Thank you," she said, and this time he actually heard her voice. "Tell Brianne that I love her. . . ."

And she was gone.

Jermyn wiped one hand across his eyes, trying not to cry. *She knew I could do it,* he thought. *She trusted me. That's a gift—something to carry with me for always. In the end, she was proud of me, as her student and maybe even as her successor as Master Spellmaker someday. Her last journeyman.*

"Gran?" Brianne said from the doorway. She moved slowly into the room, her eyes fixed on the now-mended crystal. "Gramma?"

"She's gone, Bri," he told her, taking her hands. *Of course Brianne would feel something—of course she'd come into the room just at this moment. It's only right.*

She clung to him like a very little girl. "I thought—the priest said she was at rest."

"She is," he said. "I just had to fix the crystal, so she would know it really was time to let go. She was waiting for me. The priest couldn't do that for her—it needed a spellmaker, like me. Don't worry, Brianne. Trust me."

"But—"

"Did you hear?" he asked. "She said to tell you that she loves you."

Her hands trembled in his, and she took one step forward to bury her face against his shoulder. He felt her shaking, but when she lifted her head to look at him her eyes were filled with joy.

"Thank you, Jermyn," she said simply. "Thank you—Spellmaker."

Mary Frances Zambreno is a medievalist with a love for novels of fantasy. A college teacher, she received her Ph.D. from the University of Chicago with a dissertation on medieval feasts. Ms. Zambreno also reads six languages, including Latin, French, Italian, Spanish, and Old English. However, she writes her stories in only one—English.

A lifelong resident of the Chicago area, Ms. Zambreno makes her home in the suburb of Oak Park.